PRAISE FOR *THE RIVER* AND PETER HELLER

'Urgent, visceral writing – I couldn't turn the pages fast enough. A beautiful, heartrending exploration of male friendship'
Clare Mackintosh, bestselling author of *Let Me Lie*

'Poetic and unnerving . . . A novel that sweeps you away'
USA Today

'A fiery tour de force . . . I wanted to know what happened so badly that I'd read too fast and had to retrace my steps to savour Heller's storytelling. And what a story he tells . . . I could not put this book down. It truly was terrifying and unutterably beautiful'
Denver Post

'Like his bestselling book, *The Dog Stars*, *The River* is a beauty-of-nature/cruelty-of-humanity hybrid, but this time the author leans into the thriller aspect of the tale, with gripping results . . . Heller has created indelible characters in Wynn and Jake'
Minneapolis Star Tribune

'This exquisite book made me feel so many things – terror, sorrow, excitement – and isn't that what it's all about? Heller packs a ton of adventure and emotion in this short novel, and I dare you to put it down once you've picked it up. Stunning, beautiful, life-affirming, and heart-breaking'   *Criminal Element*

'Masterly paced and artfully told, *The River* is a page-turner that demands the reader slow down and relish the sheer poetry of the language . . . Though stories of man versus nature date back to the *Odyssey*, *The River* thrills as Heller invites his characters to confront their own mortality without losing sight of the deep connections between humans and their environment'
BookPage (Starred review)

'Using an artist's eye to describe Jack and Wynn's wilderness world, *Los Angeles Times* Book Prize finalist Heller has transformed his own outdoor experiences into a heart-pounding adventure that's hard to put down'   *Library Journal* (Starred Review)

'Two college friends' leisurely river trek becomes an ordeal of fire and human malice . . . Heller confidently manages a host of tensions . . . and his pacing is masterful as well, briskly but calmly capturing the scenery in slower moments, then running full-throttle and shifting to barreling prose when danger is imminent . . . Fresh and affecting . . . An exhilarating tale delivered with the pace of a thriller and the wisdom of a grizzled nature guide'   *Kirkus* (Starred Review)

'Suspenseful . . . With its evocative descriptions of nature's splendor and brutality, Heller's novel beautifully depicts the powers that can drive humans apart – and those that compel them to return repeatedly to one another'   *Publishers Weekly*

'Heller once again chronicles life-or-death adventure with empathy for the natural world and the characters who people it. He writes most mightily of the boys' friendship and their beloved, uncompromising wilderness, depicting those layers of life that lie far beyond what is more commonly seen'   *Booklist*

'A dreamy, post-apocalyptic love letter to things of beauty, big and small'   Gillian Flynn on *The Dog Stars*

'Magical and life-affirming'   *Guardian* on *The Dog Stars*

'Like Mark Twain and Toni Morrison, Heller is a rare talent'
Elle on *Celine*

THE
RIVER

Peter Heller is a long-time contributor to NPR, and a former con-
tributing editor at *Outside Magazine*, *Men's Journal*, and *National
Geographic Adventure*. He is an award-winning adventure writer and
the author of four books of literary non-fiction and four bestselling novels, including the *New York Times* bestseller *The Dog Stars*,
a *Guardian*, *San Francisco Chronicle* and *Atlantic* Book of the Year.

Born and raised in New York, he attended Dartmouth College
in New Hampshire where he became an outdoorsman and whitewater kayaker. He has travelled the world as an expedition kayaker,
writing about challenging descents in the Pamirs, the Tien Shan
mountains, the Caucasus, Central America and Peru.

He is a graduate of the Iowa Writers' Workshop, where he
received an MFA in fiction and poetry, and won a Michener fellow-
ship for his epic poem 'The Psalms of Malvine'.

ALSO BY PETER HELLER

FICTION

Celine
The Painter
The Dog Stars

NON-FICTION

Hell or High Water: Surviving Tibet's Tsangpo River

THE
RIVER

PETER HELLER

WEIDENFELD & NICOLSON

First published in Great Britain in 2019
by Weidenfeld & Nicolson
an imprint of The Orion Publishing Group Ltd
Carmelite House, 50 Victoria Embankment
London EC4Y ODZ

An Hachette UK Company

1 3 5 7 9 10 8 6 4 2

A CIP catalogue record for this book is
available from the British Library.

ISBN (Hardback) 978 1 4746 1206 7
ISBN (Export Trade Paperback) 978 1 4746 1207 4
ISBN (eBook) 978 1 4746 1209 8
ISBN (Audio Download) 978 1 4091 8955 8

Map by Rodica Prato
Text designed by Soonyoung Kwon

Printed and bound in Great Britain by Clays Ltd, Elcograf S.p.A

www.orionbooks.co.uk
www.weidenfeldandnicolson.co.uk

To my father, John Heller,
the best storyteller I ever heard.

Who first took me out in small boats,
and who sang "Little Joe the Wrangler"
and "Barbara Allen."

THE
RIVER

They had been smelling smoke for two days.

At first they thought it was another campfire and that surprised them because they had not heard the engine of a plane and they had been traveling the string of long lakes for days and had not seen sign of another person or even the distant movement of another canoe. The only tracks in the mud of the portages were wolf and moose, otter, bear.

The winds were west and north and they were moving north so if it was another party they were ahead of them. It perplexed them because they were smelling smoke not only in early morning and at night, but would catch themselves at odd hours lifting their noses like coyotes, nostrils flaring.

And then one evening they pulled up on a wooded island and they made camp and fried a meal of lake trout on a driftwood fire and watched the sun sink into the spruce on the far shore. Late August, a clear night becoming cold. There was no aurora borealis, just the dense sparks of the stars blown from their own ancient fire. They climbed the hill. They did not need a headlamp as they were used to moving in the dark. Sometimes if they were feeling strong they paddled half the night. They loved how the darkness amplified the sounds—the gulp of the dipping paddles, the knock of the wood shaft against the gunwale. The long desolate cry of a loon. The loons especially. How they hollowed out the night with longing.

Tonight there was no loon and almost no wind and they went up through tamarack and hemlock and a few large birch trees whose pale bark fluoresced. At the top of the knoll they followed a game trail to a ledge of broken rock as if they weren't the first who had sought the view. And they saw it. They looked northwest. At first they thought it was the sun, but it was far too late for any lingering sunset and there were no cities in that direction for a thousand miles. In the farthest distance, over the trees, was an orange glow. It lay on the horizon like the light from banked embers and it fluttered barely so they wondered if it was their eyes and they knew it was a fire.

A forest fire, who knew how far off or how big, but bigger than any they could imagine. It seemed to spread over two quadrants and they didn't say a word but the silence of it and the way it seemed to breathe scared them to the bone. The prevailing wind would push the blaze right to them. At the pace they were going they were at least two weeks from the Cree village of Wapahk and Hudson Bay. When the most northerly lake spilled into the river they would pick up speed but there was no way to shorten the miles.

~

On the morning after seeing the fire they did spot another camp. It was on the northeastern verge of a wooded island and they swung out to it and were surprised that no one was breaking down the large wall tent. No one was going anywhere. There was an old white-painted square-stern woodstrip canoe on the gravel with a trolling motor clamped to the transom and two men in folding lawn chairs, legs sprawled straight. Jack and Wynn beached and hailed them and the men lifted their arms. They had a plastic fifth of Ancient Age bourbon on the stones between the chairs. The heavier one wore a flannel shirt and square steel-rimmed tinted glasses, the skinny one a Texans cap. Two spinning rods and a Winchester Model 70 bolt-action rifle leaned against a pine.

Jack said, "You-all see the fire?"

The skinny one said, "You-all see any pussy?" The men burst out laughing. They were drunk. Jack felt disgust, but being drunk on a summer morning didn't deserve a death sentence.

Jack said, "There's a fire. Big-ass fire to the northwest. What you've been smelling the last few days."

Wynn said, "You guys have a satellite phone?"

That set them off again. When they were finished laughing, the heavy one said, "You two need to chillax. Whyn't you pull up a chair." There were no extra chairs. He lifted the bourbon by the neck between two fingers and rocked it toward them. Jack held up a hand and the man shrugged and brought the fifth up, watching its progress intently as though he was operating a crane. He drank. The lake was a narrow reach and if the fire overran the western shore this island would not keep the men safe.

"How've you been making the portages?" Jack said. He meant the carries between the lakes. There were five lakes, stringing south to north. Some of the lakes were linked by channels of navigable river, others by muddy trails that necessitated unloading everything and carrying. The last lake flowed into the river. It was a big river that meandered generally north a hundred and fifty miles to the Cree village and the bay. Jack was not impressed with the men's fitness level.

"We got the wheely thing," the skinny man said. He made a sweeping gesture at the camp.

"We got just about everything," the fat man said.

"Except pussy." The two let out another gust of laughter.

Jack said, "The fire's upwind. There. We figure maybe thirty miles off. It's a killer."

The fat man brought them into focus. His face turned serious. "We got it covered," he said. "Do you? It's all copacetic here. Whyn't you have a drink?" He gestured at Wynn. "You, the big one—what's your name?"

"Wynn."

"He's the mean one, huh?" The fat man cocked his head at Jack. "What's his name? Go Home? Win or Go Home. Ha!"

Wynn didn't know what to say. Jack looked at them. He said, "Well, you might get to high ground and take a look thataway one evening." He pointed across the lake. He didn't think either of them would climb a hill or a tree. He waved, wished them luck without conviction, and he and Wynn got in their canoe and left.

~

On the third day after seeing the fire they were paddling the east shore of a lake called Blueberries. What it said on the map, and it was an odd name and no way to make it sound right. Blueberries Lake. They were paddling close to shore because the wind was up and straight out of the west and rocking them badly. It was a strange morning: a hard frost early that lingered and then the wind rose up and the black waves piled into them nearly broadside, rank on rank. The tops of the whitecaps blew into the sides of their faces and the waves lapped over the port gunwale so that they decided to surf into a cobble beach and they snapped on the spray deck that covered the open canoe. But there was fog, too. The wind tore into a dense mist and did not blow it away. Neither of them had ever seen anything like it.

They were paddling close to shore and they heard shouting. At first they thought it was birds or wolves. They didn't know what. As with the fire, they could not at first countenance the cause. Human voices were the last thing they expected but that's what it was. A man shouting and a woman's remonstra-tion, high and angry. The cries shredded in the wind. Wynn half turned in the bow and pointed with his paddle, but only for a second as they needed speed for headway or they would capsize. His gesture was a question: Should we stop?

An hour before, when they had beached to put on the spray skirt, they had landed hard. Wynn was heavier and having his weight in front had helped in the wind, but then they had surfed a wave into shore and thwomped onto the rocks, which thankfully were smooth; if the beach had been limestone shale they would have broken the boat. It was a dangerous maneuver.

They could not make out the words, but the woman sounded furious and the man did not sound menacing, just outraged. Jack shook his head. A couple might expect privacy in their home, why shouldn't they be granted the same in the middle of nowhere? They could not see the figures or even the shore, but now and then there was an intimation of trees, just a shadow in the tearing fog, a dark wall which they knew was the edge of the forest, and they paddled on.

CHAPTER ONE

The two of them loved paddling in storm. With the spray deck sealing the canoe they felt safe as long as they did not broach sideways, and they struck out away from the shadows and sounds of shore. The compass heading was redundant as long as they kept the breaking waves on the port quarter. They could take heavy water but a capsize away from land would kill them, so they were very careful to power through the whitecaps at an angle. They both paddled on their knees to keep the center of gravity low. It was exhausting. Then the wind died all at once as if throttled and in less than half an hour the lake glassed off and they felt suspended in fog. They moved within a moving nimbus in which only a few yards of black water were visible in any direction, and the pale fog drifted in tatters like stubborn smoke. The water whispered along the hull and it had a silver sheen that reminded Wynn of rayon. All of it was dreamlike; he thought of a Poe novel he had read in which the castaways are pulled toward the South Pole and the current they are riding gets warmer and calmer as they go.

Wynn stopped paddling. As the bowman today he set the pace and so Jack quit paddling too and they glided. The boat was sleek Kevlar, nineteen feet, and with a V'd hull in bow and stern it glided straight. There was something satisfying in a cessation of paddling on smooth water. It was like watching a flock of ducks all stop beating at once and sail over a bank of trees on extended wings.

"That was weird," Jack said.

"Fucking A. Which part?"

"I can tick them off," Jack said. He set the paddle across the spray deck and pried a tin of Skoal out of his shirt's breast pocket. He was soaked from spray, but Jack never wore a rain jacket when he was paddling because he said he got just as wet from sweat, even in the breathable stuff. He also didn't use bug dope, on principle. He tucked a pinch into his lip. "Let's see: Wind and fog together, that's a first. Oh yeah, and frost. The sudden calm. The shouts. And this. This is kinda weird."

Wynn didn't say anything. They were still gliding and something about the near silence was like a sacrament. He stuck a finger in the dark water and it was still cold, probably near forty degrees, and he watched his finger cut a small V-wake. It was the only sure sign of motion. "I was thinking of that story by Poe," he said finally. *Arthur Gordon Pym.*

"Yeah, right?" Jack spat. "I wonder who they were. It sounded like a couple."

"Maybe we'll see them again."

"I hope not. All morning I've been wondering if we should've stopped."

"To tell them about the fire?"

"Yeah."

"It would've been dicey," Wynn said. He meant to surf in—and what if the beach had been broken limestone? They called any open shoreline that ran smoothly to the water a beach.

Jack said, "I was thinking maybe we should have stopped and tried to hail them."

They drifted. "Want some lunch?" Wynn said.

"Okay. I guess we're good with the deck."

They unbuttoned the spray deck from its cleats and Jack rummaged in the day bag and pulled out a brick of sharp cheddar, a dry summer sausage, and a Ziploc full of half-broken Triscuits. He sat up on the cane seat. There was a small cutting board in the bag, too, and Jack flipped open his clip knife and set the board on his knees and sliced the cheese and sausage.

~

They were best friends at Dartmouth who had decided to take the summer and fall quarters off. They had worked as wilderness instructors for an outdoor program in the Adirondacks all June and July, and they decided to blow half their savings on the flights in and out of the river in the old Otter floatplane. Neither was attached. Jack had broken up with his high school sweetheart in the spring. She lived in the Fraser valley of Colorado, near Granby, where Jack's family had their small ranch.

Wynn had not had a girl since junior year at the Putney School in Vermont. It was kind of a fancy boarding school, but his family lived three miles away and he was a day student. He'd dated the daughter of a movie star, who'd found him exotic and rustic, and he told Jack he had known it wouldn't work when he went home with her to Malibu during spring break and they'd all gone out to brunch on a weekday and the star mother and the daughter ordered eggs Florentine and he'd asked what it was and both their heads swiveled and the mother said, "Wynn, it's like Benedict but with spinach instead of Canadian bacon." She'd adjusted her glasses. "Benedict?" she'd said. "Yes? No?" and they'd both burst out laughing and Keri had reached over and patted him on the shoulder. He knew what eggs Benedict was. He said the pat burned like a brand and that afternoon he'd changed his flight and flown home. It was sugaring season anyway, one of his favorite times, and he helped his father boil in the little sugar shack along Sawyer Brook.

Sometimes they boiled all night. At dawn the sun washed the patchy snow in a rose light, and the daybreak wind rattled the dried leaves of the oaks and the bare branches of the maples, and he heard the rush of the snowmelt brook, the songs of the nuthatch. The fire crackled under the long pan of clear sap and he and his dad didn't say much, but he was aware enough— he'd read enough fiction, he guessed—to realize that these might be the best hours he and his father ever spent together.

He also came to see in the long hours of trying to work through his heartache that maybe he had been just as ruthlessly shallow and opportunistic as she had been: she'd wanted to indulge in a local boy who wore flannel shirts and could fish and cut wood and was as at home sleeping under the stars as she was in a five-star suite, and he'd wanted to date the daughter of a star who moved through the world like a different species. But really she was just a young girl who was far from home and probably scared, and he was much more cultured than he let on and had spent more hours in the art museums of Boston and New York than he cared to admit. He just had never had eggs Florentine.

He came to the conclusion one morning walking the sugar-bush of Dusty Ridge that he and Keri had never really been friends and that they had rarely laughed. That was sad.

Jack's story was simpler. He had known Cheryl since second grade, when her father came to the valley to take over as police chief, and they were best friends, and now she wanted to get married and have kids and he realized that she was the best kind of woman and that he was already bored. He'd written her the Dear Jill letter in May, and when he'd said he hoped they remained friends forever he meant it.

So both Jack and Wynn had digested their share of bewilderment, and maybe there was a heavy place like a stone inside each of them. Wynn would never admit that he'd been in love and that Keri's scorn had been a gut punch. Or that maybe he hadn't dated in the first two years of college because he was gun-shy.

They drifted. Jack kept slicing the cheese and the sausage until there was none left. They ate like wolves. The good thing about a canoe trip is that they didn't have to be shy about provisions.

They had two three-foot plastic barrels stuffed with enough food probably to get by even if they never caught another fish.

"They must be paddling down to Wapahk," Jack said. That was the village they were headed for: the plan was to paddle this last lake that emptied into the river, then the river for a couple of weeks, then take out at the little settlement at the mouth of Hudson Bay.

"Or they're just paddling the lakes up here and they'll get picked up. Them and the drunks."

They thought about that. It occurred to them, though neither of them spoke it, that with the fire coming the safest thing would be to catch a flight out of Blueberries Lake. They'd flown in to the first lake on floats and they could take off on them, too. Because this evening or tomorrow morning this most northerly lake would pour into a river. And when they left the lake behind and paddled into the tongue of current that became the Maskwa there would be no going back. They would ride the swift V of moving water into the channel and they would be committed to paddling all the way to Hudson Bay. There would be nowhere on the large but constricted river to land a floatplane until they were near the mouth in two weeks. But. They could not stay up on the lake because they had no radio or sat phone to contact the airfield in Pickle Lake for a pickup—or any airfield. Or anyone, if they needed a rescue. They'd talked about it in planning the trip and decided that modern communications had made true adventure a thing of the past. Plus, they couldn't afford a sat phone.

They drifted in the fog. The lightest breeze from the northwest carried the sharp scent that was different from the smell of the woodstoves, which was so familiar in the valleys where they had grown up. It was heavier with char and smelled darker somehow.

"Maybe they have a phone," Wynn ventured. They drifted.

Jack said, "You think we should abort?"

Wynn shrugged.

They had paddled many rivers together in the two years they'd known each other, and climbed a lot of peaks. Sometimes one had more appetite for danger, sometimes the other. There was a delicate but strong balance of risk versus caution in their team thinking, with the roles often fluid, and it's what made them such good partners. Jack would not disrespect his friend by belittling his concern. He said, "We've made a lot of effort to get here, huh?"

"Yep."

"But nobody wants to get overrun by a megafire."

"Nope."

"Want a chocolate bar?" Jack said.

"Sure."

They could barely feel the breeze on their left ears and cheeks and it moved the fog over the water with a timeless languor as if there never had been a time without fog and there would never be one again. It seemed to be lightening.

"If they aren't getting picked up and they are planning to head downriver, we should tell the couple about the fire," Wynn said. He handed his wrapper to Jack, who crumpled it and tucked it into a mesh pocket slung on one of the barrels. They'd burn the wrappers tonight. "Everyone going downriver is going to want to hustle."

Jack blew through his cheeks. "We'll lose half a day, huh?" He picked up his paddle from where he'd slid it into the pocket of the bow.

"Yep."

"Well, let's lose it then."

They spun the canoe against the light resistance of the false keel, spun it on the smooth water as if on a spindle, and straightened out and dug in. Back the way they had come. Without the wind and waves to provide the angle of a heading, Jack used the compass and held a course of 170 degrees and they paddled back into the mist to warn the other party.

～

The fog did lift. It seemed to lighten and clear within minutes, vanishing into the crisp morning as if it had never existed, and the sky was cloudless and an autumn blue. The clarity of the air was like putting on magnifying glasses: every trunk of every birch tree seemed to stand out against the backdrop of tamarack, of spruce, and there were touches of yellow at the edges of the limbs, and some of the tamarack needles were the faded colors of fall grass. The pink fireweed along the shore beneath the trees popped as in a painting. Overnight it seemed summer had surrendered to fall. It was beautiful and it scared them both. All the whitewater was ahead of them, and it would be much safer if the warmer days of late summer persisted. They had brought wetsuits, but they'd heard about expeditions getting overrun by early snow or cold and men dying. It had happened on a now-famous canoe trip of six Dartmouth men in 1955 up on the Dubawnt when the leader, named Art Moffatt, had died after a long swim through a rapid in freezing weather. Up here there was no predicting the timing of the seasons and they had picked their window for the chance of lowest water and warmest days; also, it was when their jobs had ended.

They paddled. Jack hummed. He usually hummed when he paddled, bars of old cowboy songs his father had sung to him like "Streets of Laredo" and "Little Joe the Wrangler" and "Barbara Allen." Also Sky Ferreira and Drake and Solange; Wynn appreciated the range.

A few days back they had been paddling between two islands on Lake Sorrow and Wynn in the stern had seen something in the water. It was big and it was cutting a wake like a small boat. He stared. Whatever it was, it was traveling toward the same island on which they'd planned to make camp. Jack was humming and partly singing in snatches Wyclef Jean's "Guantanamera": "I'm standing at the bar smoking a Cuban cigar . . . Hey yo I think she's eyein' me from afar . . ." Wynn squinted in the stern and made out the rack of a moose. Huge. It must have been, it looked big even from that distance. Two miles from the nearest shore. Great. They'd be sharing a little island with a comfortably amphibious bull moose. At least it wasn't rut season yet. "Hey, hey Jack, look at that. Damn." He didn't know why he was whispering. Jack kept humming, lost in some reverie. *"Hey."* Hum, murmur, a snatch of rap. "Hey! *Dude!*" Jack had turned, startled.

"Do you know you hum all day?"

"I do?"

"Yep. And we're gonna have company." Wynn pointed with his paddle.

"Crap, is that a *moose*?" Jack laughed. "Too bad we can't harness the fucker like a reindeer. Look at him haul the mail. Must be going four knots."

They had decided to camp on the island anyway and had no problem coexisting that night. The south shore had a cove full of duckweed and they'd walked around quietly and watched him feed. Just before full dark they'd been sitting at the fire drinking late coffee and Jack had whistled soundless and Wynn had turned and they saw the moose standing at the edge of the woods watching, and he seemed forlorn, as if he wanted to join them. He had clearly never seen a human before.

Now, with the fog lifted and the air lens-clear and cold, they thought they'd have no problem spotting the couple's camp, but they couldn't. It occurred to them that maybe there'd been more than two. Two people. Maybe it had been an entire expedition camped on the east shore and all they'd heard was the shouting of the couple down on the beach. Maybe the man and the woman had walked away from the group to argue. But then it would have been even easier to spot the colorful tents of this other party, or to see the string of canoes making their way north to the lake's outlet and the true river, but they didn't. They didn't see a thing.

They saw the patches of bright fireweed and the wall of woods, and shallow bays with stony beaches sometimes backed by fringes of tall tawny grass; they saw rocky coves with deadfall spruce lying across black boulders and bleached like bones, and low patches of vegetation between the rocks on the shore that they knew were lowbush blueberries.

If they were tempted to stop and pick they didn't say it. They were feeling pressured now. What they had wanted by giving themselves almost a month, more, to cross the lakes and run the river was a voyage with no hard end date. They left the flight out from Wapahk open-ended—they'd call when they got to the village—and they'd planned a leisurely pace with short days whenever they wanted. With layovers in camp to hike, to hunt if they felt like it, to forage for berries, to rest and smoke their pipes and take their ease like Huck Finn or Stubb—the pipes were anachronistic and they loved them, to recline in camp and puff a vanilla tobacco mix made them feel like old explorers. They hungered to immerse themselves in the country without the hurry of a jammed itinerary. They'd even left their watches, trusting their sense of time to the sun and stars when they could see them and to their bodies' rhythms when they couldn't. Most of their previous river trips had been a hustle, because they were students with jobs and so their time off was short. They wanted to try this, to feel what it was actually like to live in the landscape a little. But now everything had changed. The fire they'd seen the other night and the early frost had changed it.

They paddled back a hundred and seventy degrees from the way they'd come, which angled them toward shore, and they thought it was odd that they hadn't seen any sign of a recent camp or crossed tracks with another canoe. A small tributary creek wound out of the woods and across a broader beach and they decided to stop and make a fire and have tea and think about things. Normally they might have fished the side slough but now they didn't. It was a darker color than the lake which had hued to an opaque green in the early-afternoon sun. The creek was brown with tannin, and they'd often had luck catching brookies in the smaller tributaries, but neither of them pulled out his rod.

There was plenty of wood. They were on the leeward shore and the driftwood wracked up on the stone beach like the flotsam of a tide line. There were the skeletons of fir trees that silvered smooth and hard, and the carcasses of birch that rotted, still sheathed in their skins of powdery white bark. Piles of smaller sticks seasoned in the sun and wind and they cracked over Jack's knee like a gunshot. He gathered an armload while Wynn stood in his rubber Wellington boots a few feet into the water and scanned with his binocs up and down the shore and over the jade water toward the mouth of the outlet. Jack noticed that he often did that—stood a foot deep in the shallows when he could just as easily have stood on shore—and it amused him. Just as Jack was comfortable with heights and exposure, Wynn loved to be immersed whenever he could, and never minded the chaos of whitewater—it's when he seemed to come most alive. The same for fishing: Jack would rather fish a river from the dry bow of an oar boat, while Wynn preferred to be thigh-deep in a stiff current and wading. Jack chalked it up to landscapes of origin—he was raised in the heart of the Rocky Mountains and that's where he was comfortable. High desert, higher peaks. Wynn's world had been a country of brooks and rivers, ponds, lakes; a world of water.

Wynn kept a finger on the focus knob and moved the binocs over the northern shore. He could not actually see the cut where the lake emptied but he knew where it was from the map. It was beside the hump of a glacial moraine that in another epoch had been a pile of tumbled rocks and was now softened with moss and trees. They had been so close to it earlier in the morning and it was now about five miles distant. It's where the river started, and a mile and a half down the river were the first big falls, a terrible stepped rapid that had killed four canoers last year who had missed the mandatory portage on river right. But it was very swift water above the drop and the left bank was a sheer ledge with no place to pull out. One of the biggest warnings in any description of the entire river was to be far to the right in the mile below the lake.

A pair of mergansers winged into the field of Wynn's glasses and out of it, beating fast southward. He scanned east and caught a big raptor circling; he followed it and it flashed white and he was sure it was a bald eagle hunting.

But no canoe. Wynn gave up, and Jack knew what he was going to do next and he did. He set the binocs on the rocks where they wouldn't dangle off his neck and then he squatted and began prospecting for stones up and down the beach. He gathered armloads. Not just rocks but sticks, two feathers, probably osprey and crow—and he knelt and stacked the stones into two piles, less like cairns than funeral mounds, and channeled the water around them and lay the feathers in the channels like boats. "Longboats," he muttered to himself, but Jack heard him. "Like a Viking funeral." If Jack hummed, Wynn talked to himself, especially while making his Thingamajigs. What Jack called them. Wynn was crazy about Goldsworthy, the environmental sculptor, and was in awe of the ethic of ephemeral art, from Buddhist sandpainting to the sapling moons of Jay Mead. The untethering of ego: the purity of creating something that wouldn't even be around to sign in a matter of hours or days. What that said about ownership and the impermanence of all things. He was less impressed with the extravagant shroudings of Christo, which he thought were grandiose and domineering.

Squatting there at water's edge, Wynn reminded Jack of a little kid at the beach with a bucket and pail. He was just as absorbed and happy. "Aren't you even going to take a picture?"

Wynn looked up, shrugged. He had a goofy smile, like someone caught in the act of talking seriously to a chipmunk.

Jack started a fire. It popped and blazed and he dipped the kettle and arranged two flat rocks beside the flames and with a stick he raked coals and burning sticks into the gap, over which he placed the pot. The water boiled fast and he flipped up the wire handle with his stick and lifted it onto one of the rocks and went to the canoe and dug tea and brown sugar from a plastic box they used as a day bag. There were two emergency blankets and waterproof matches and a tube of firestarter in the bottom of it. And a packet of food, rolled oats and sugar, power bars, freeze-dried fruit, and a few meals; enough for maybe three days for the two of them. Also a signaling mirror and a small compass with no bezel. He dropped the tea bags into the kettle and sat on a smooth log in the bright sun and watched the lake.

There is no place I'd rather be, he thought. And also: Something is not right. He could feel it on the back of his neck, almost the way the hair prickles and rises just before a lightning storm in the Never Summers back home. Just before he stepped into a Montana clearing straight into the glare of a grizzly. He'd always had it, that sixth sense—some people do—and he thought it had saved his bacon more than once. He'd had it the morning he was eleven and a young mare had stumbled on the slick rock of an angled slab above a raging summer creek. Now he felt the heat rise in his neck and he shoved the image away.

He breathed. Nothing more peaceful, he thought, than right now. He could hear bees humming in the fireweed and asters behind him. The tea was brewing, the lake glassed off, a white sun hung midway to the woods and warmed the stony shore. His clothes were almost completely dry. His best friend was thirty feet away, evidently just as content. *Nothing better than this.* What he liked to say to himself.

There was no plume of smoke to the west, the wind there must have shifted. Here there was barely any breeze, the pale smoke of their fire stirred almost straight upward and thinned and vanished before it reached the height of the spruce. But it bothered him, the feeling. They should be now very close to the place on the shore where they'd heard the shouting and there was nothing, no sign.

He poured the two stainless travel mugs full of the steeped tea and shook brown sugar into his and stirred it with a twig and sat on his log and couldn't relax. What had been sheer fun before now felt ominous. The foreboding didn't feel like a general threat, like *Fall is coming early, we better hustle,* or *There's a big fucking fire to the northwest and we might want to pick up our pace*—he was used to those shifts. In a ranching family they happened on an almost daily basis and he had learned to set them in a place in his psyche that did not disturb his daily well-being—life was about being agile in spirit and adapting quickly. This was different. It prickled on his skin like a specific and imminent danger which he could not place.

"Hey," he said. "Ding-ding. Tea's ready."

Wynn stood and picked up the binocs. He tromped up to the fire and sat on the log. Jack handed him his cup of tea. "Strange," Wynn said. "I scanned the whole shore. You don't think it could've been the wind? What we heard?"

"What? The wind shouting, 'This is *my* goddamn trip. This time it's *mine!*' That's what I thought I heard."

"Yeah. Me, too. That was her. I thought I heard him yell, 'Bullshit! I'm through! This is the last time!'"

"What do you want to do?" They'd paddled over ten miles already.

"You?"

"Well." Jack studied the stones between his feet and moved his jaw around. Wynn knew that's what he did when he was thinking hard. "They might have passed us somehow in the fog. Unlikely, though, huh?"

They were both exceptionally strong paddlers and they knew it, and that morning in the waves they weren't holding back.

"Like they might have an electric motor and a solar panel like those jackasses."

"They could have," Jack said. "People bring them just for crossing the lakes."

"Man. Why not just stay home and drive around?" Wynn was more of a purist than Jack. A few times that morning Jack had thought having a motor would've been awesome.

Jack said, "It feels funny, though. I don't know."

"Is that your Spidey sense talking?"

"Yep."

"Damn!" Wynn jerked away the cup and spilled tea onto the stones. "I always do that." He unscrewed the cap on his mug and blew on the piping-hot tea. "Burned my tongue."

Jack barely heard him. He was wrestling with a rare sense of portent. He said, "Whoever it was, it feels like we did our due diligence. We tried to warn them."

Jack didn't want to throw shadow onto the trip; there was nothing worse on any expedition than a naysayer. But now he kind of wished they had found whoever it was and that they'd had a sat phone and they could call into Pickle Lake. Maybe not for a plane, but at least for an update on the fire, which he was sure the Fire Center must be monitoring.

The hair standing up on the back of his neck, the goose-bumps, he'd learned not to ignore them. It was almost like a distant ringing of alarm bells somewhere deep at the base of his skull, which he could hear if he listened. But they didn't have a sat phone and the couple was nowhere and they'd already made their decision to leave the lake and enter the river. Which was a funnel of current and committed them to two weeks at least of swift water and portages around bigger rapids. He didn't say a word; this time he kept his mouth shut.

"Wanna make camp here?" Wynn said. "That'll give us plenty of time tomorrow to get across and down to the falls, and we can take our time and be really careful."

"Okay. Hey, Big One?"

"Yeah?"

"Nothing."

Wynn lowered his tea and studied the side of his friend's face. Under the week of beard the prominent cheekbones were deeply tanned, the straight nose sunburned, the crow's feet at the corner of his almost black eye a spray of fine wrinkles, paler than the skin around them; his tendoned neck was smattered with small sun spots. He hadn't earned any of those learning to canoe at summer camp or attending the National Outdoor

Leadership School. Wynn envied him. He thought again how being outside, sleeping under stars, cooking on a fire, were as natural to Jack as breathing. He'd been on horse pack trips with his family ever since he could cling to the back of a green-broke mare. And he didn't seem to mind being cold and wet or exhausted the way other people did. It wasn't fun, but then life wasn't meant to be that fun. That was the difference, Wynn thought. For Jack, stuff like cold and hunger didn't have a value, good or bad, they just were, and it was best if they didn't last that long; but if they did, as long as one survived them, no harm, no foul. It gave Jack a strength, a temper, that Wynn admired. At about five-ten, Jack was almost six inches shorter than Wynn. Wynn could grunt a car out of the mud, but Jack was lighter and leaner and could run faster, and Wynn knew he had that toughness that was bred in the bone. So when Jack was troubled, Wynn paid attention.

"What are you thinking, Cap?"

Jack shrugged.

"You've got a bad feeling?"

"Maybe a little."

"Me, too. The fire, and those guys were creeps. It's all gotten weird. But we don't have much choice, do we?"

Jack turned his head. In the bright sun his dark eyes were clear and full of lights. If he was worried, he was also partly amused. At how shit stacked up. "Nope, we don't," he said. "Which means we don't have to decide a thing."

~

They had plenty of staples, black bean powder and quinoa, rice, macaroni, lentils, even pounds of jerky. They had also brought some fancy premade freeze-dried meals for variety and relief, and they decided that night to make turkey à la king. They ate it with relish, and Wynn mixed lemonade powder in a water bottle and they poured it into their cups and added a splash of Jim Beam from a plastic flask. There's always relief in committing to a decision, even when there's no choice.

Neither of them understood why it was called turkey à la king. Wynn pointed out that it seemed to be French and *king* was masculine and so it should be *le* king. Jack said that *à la* is like the *au* in *au gratin,* meaning "made with," which must mean that there were bits of the king in the food. He admitted that it had been his favorite meal at Granby Public Schools.

They pitched the tent in a cove of spruce off the beach. Neither of them felt like fishing, though they saw fry darting in the tea-colored shallows of the creek. They read and smoked their pipes. What wind there was died to a breath they could barely feel. The sky was clear and cloudless. The last light slid down to the edges and slipped onto the silvered lake which bore it without a ruffle. Also the reflections of the first stars. The cold came on fast and they knew it would be another night of frost.

They kicked up the fire and added driftwood and sat in the heat. Wynn pulled out the pages he had torn from a book called *True Tales of the North: Ghosts, Witches, Spirit Bears, and Windigoes.* It was written in 1937 by an amateur anthropologist named Spencer Halberd Knight. Jack had teased Wynn about the name—"If that's on the sonofabitch's birth certificate I'll eat that chapter"—and about Wynn's habit of tearing books apart for his trips—"You must've grown up with a hell of a lot more books than I did. Whyn't you just let them live out their natural life?"—but he'd asked sheepishly if he could read the pages when Wynn was done. The wood was dry and burned bright and Wynn turned sideways on the log they'd pulled over for a seat and scanned the first page.

"I was telling you, there's a whole chapter on Wapahk. That's some dark history up there."

"Yeah?" Jack feigned nonchalance, but he was sitting up. There was nothing he loved more than a good dark story.

"A whole string of murders in the twenties. This gaunt pale giant spirit haunted the village and possessed people and turned them into cannibals. It was called the Windigo. So what happened is, whenever the elders thought a villager was possessed by the Windigo they shot or strangled him so he couldn't eat his friends and family. Kind of a preemptive strike."

"How many?"

Wynn turned farther away from the fire so the light fell on the text. "Nine. In a village of maybe two hundred."

"Damn."

"I know."

"Maybe it was a starving polar bear."

"Maybe." Jack sounded to Wynn a little like a kid desperate for an explanation.

"One of those that likes to walk on two legs."

"Huh."

"Could've been a bad seal year for some reason," Jack suggested.

"Could've been. Says the village felt doubly cursed because warm currents made the fishing bad two years in a row."

Jack felt goosebumps for the second time that day. "Well, what the hell do you think it was?"

"A hungry ghost."

"Fuck you."

The campfire quieted to embers and they could not smell the conflagration in the northwest at all; it was as if it no longer existed. The breeze must have backed around. They didn't talk about it but now and then each turned his face sideways to the lake and flared nostrils exactly like an elk or deer would, scenting for a predator.

An hour after full dark they turned in and left the door of the tent unzipped and tied back so that they could see the stars, and the northern lights if they sang silently later on. They closed the mesh screen so it would collect the frost. Later Jack moved his pad and bag out onto the cobbles of the beach and slept under the throbbing arch of the Milky Way. He didn't care about the frost, it would feather on his bag and he could shake it off in the morning. Last night's freeze had taken care of the mosquitoes. Wynn heard the knock of stone as Jack moved outside, and he also heard the slow creek making the faintest ripple. He thought of the Merwin poem about dusk that he loved so much. Merwin describes the sun going down believing in nothing, and how he hears the stream running after it: *It has brought its flute it is a long way.*

It killed him. The one and only sun without belief in anything and the little stream believing so hard, believing in music even. What he loved about poetry: it could do in a few seconds what a novel did in days. A painting could be like that, too, and a sculpture. But sometimes you wanted something to take days and days.

Jack lay awake for a long time and when he slept he dreamed of his mother and the morning on the Encampment. He had the same dream a few times a year. They camped in Horseshoe Park, the meadow beneath the little bridge, just as they had in real life. There were just the three of them—his father, he, and his mom—just as it had been, and when they broke camp his father rode Dandy, his favorite hunting horse, and led BJ, the strawberry roan mare who was half Arab and who they always used as a packhorse because she was too twitchy to ride. She could rear at a chipmunk or leap over a low deadfall stick as if it were a two-rail jump.

The trail ran into the spruce along the right bank of the river. The river still rushed with snowmelt in late June. It was really just a big creek and it dropped fast into a constricted

shaded canyon densely wooded with spruce and pine. The
trail climbed away from the thundering rapids. His mother
rode ahead of him on Mindy, a sweet, big-boned quarter-horse
mare, and he followed on Duke, his young gray. In the dream,
and as it had been that morning, he insisted on taking up the
rear, it made him feel more grown-up. As in real life they took
their time. The trail was narrow and rocky and it hugged the
side of the steep slope. His father sang as he rode. Fifty feet
below, the river cliffed out into a narrow rock-walled gorge and
vanished in a sharp right bend. The whitewater roared up like
a jet engine and sent mist into the trees. His heart hammered
and he loved this. His father in the lead got to a short sloping slab of bedrock and clucked Dandy across it. Jack heard
the grating strike of the steel shoes, saw BJ toss her head, put
her nose down and cross, he heard the bit rings jangle and
the dainty click of her steps, and then his mother urged the
slow-gaited Mindy, *Good girl, what a sweet girl.* As in real life
something spooked BJ just ahead and she balked back and
tautened the lead and his father, who held the line, called,
"Whoa, girl! Easy!" and Mindy bunched back, she was on the
slick slab and her rear hoof slid. The rear left foot, Jack saw it
right there beneath him, the shod hoof slipped and scrambled
for purchase, his mother yelling, "Hey, girl!"—the butt of the
horse sliding and now the fore hooves scrabbled at the mossy
bank above the trail and—he saw it all as if in slow motion,
the horse, and his mother still reining and leaning forward
over her mane trying to save the mare, and she lost all trac-
tion, flailing the back legs now and the mare screamed as she
went over. Not his mother, the mare. A scream like a terrified
human. He saw them hit a large spruce and get knocked sideways and out and they separated in air, his mother still clutch-
ing the reins, her hat knocked into space and tumbling like a

shot bird, that moment frozen before it wasn't and they hit the white torrent together. For a moment, miraculously, they were swimming, she was grabbing for the saddle, then they went over what must have once been a ledge but was now the hump of a breaking wave that rolled down into the trench of a thundering backward-breaking hydraulic, they vanished, came up once, first the mare's dark head, then his mother's arm before they slammed into the wall and were tugged around the bend. His father when he could speak shouted, "Stay!" and he looked wildly back and yelled, "Can you hold him? *Can you?*" and Jack nodded, mute, and his father let go the lead line of his packhorse and spurred Dandy into a crazy lunge down the trail. He was gone. In real life they both were gone. BJ loped after his father, trailing the rope. Jack stayed. He reined tight the quivering gelding and they were both shaking and he stayed. He would do what his father demanded. He loved her more than anything on earth. He was eleven.

But in the dream her hat caught itself and took wing and flew up to the other side of the canyon and caught the sunlight like a turning hawk, and she and Mindy did not hit the white rush but floated a moment in air and he knew they would figure out how to fly, too, he knew it, and when he woke up under the late stars a loon was calling pitched and lonely somewhere far out and the pillow of his jacket was wet and he knew he'd been crying again.

~

Jack woke before sunrise and shook off his frost-covered bag in a spray of snowflakes that floated for a moment like an icy hatch of mayflies. He started a fire and put coffee on while

Wynn slept or read. Nothing on earth he loved more than to be the first one up, cracking sticks for a fire, making coffee.

The lake was still, a pale half-moon setting over the fringe of trees. He found the tin of Skoal in his shirt pocket and had his first chew sitting on the log and watching the flames lick blue along the lengths of driftwood, catching and flaring. He tried not to think about the dream. Except he did think that the mare Mindy must have taken wing somehow, in real life, was somehow transported out of the certain death of that white funnel, because that morning a fishing guide scouting the trail for July clients saw her scramble out of a riffle onto the right bank and stand wild-eyed and shaking. She was cut and bruised, she had a deep gash along her right flank and a sprained fetlock, but she was otherwise okay. A miracle if there ever was such a thing on earth. She fully recovered, but would never again walk a river trail. His mother wasn't so lucky. He stopped the thought. He looked out over the water that held the bruised rose and grays of dawn. Well. Few people had the luck to die in the prime of life in full appreciation of all the goodness therein. Leave it at that, he thought. As good a place as any.

They hadn't caught any fish, so he mixed up some powdered egg with chunks of cheddar and oiled the long-handled pan and then threw stones at the tent until Wynn groaned and got up.

CHAPTER TWO

The canoe moved this morning as if greased. North again toward the top of the lake where it became a true river. They let their eyes rove the shore looking for the colors of a tent or tents, the shape of a boat on a beach, but saw only more patches of yellow in the trees and a swath of orange black-eyed Susans on the shore. They watched a skein of geese fly over that end of the lake, just one side of the V, an uneven phalanx that curved and straightened as they flew in constant correction. The distant barks drifted down. Jack thought how nature was so often imperfect and sometimes perplexed or bewildered. Once on Duke he had ridden up on a golden eagle in a sage meadow who had just feasted on a prairie dog and the huge bird hopped and tried to fly and was too heavy with her meal. She turned and stood tall and glared at them, awaiting her fate, which was only the indignity of hearing Jack laugh.

They didn't smell the big fire this morning and they wondered if it had damped down, somehow died off in the new cold. Then they could relax again.

"It'd be good to see it," Jack said. "To check one more time before we get on the river."

"Yeah it would."

"Wanna pull out and climb a tree or something?"

"That'd be you."

"Never a question," Jack said.

They pulled out on the west side of the cut and the outflow. The thin strand of stones was partly shadowed by tamarack and grown over by a stand of stiff dried mullein, the tall stalks that Jack's dad called cowboy candlestick. White moths flitted in and out of the sunlight and lighted on the purple asters that edged the beach. The boys climbed up the low moraine covered in trees and they chose a tall straight balsam fir. Wynn laced his fingers and boosted Jack to where he could reach the first limb.

It was just big enough to bear his weight, and he grasped it close to the trunk and chinned up and reached for the next and was climbing. A few needles spun down, as did his curses. It wasn't that he was barking his arms while shinnying or gumming his hair and face with bubbles of sap—he was, but he didn't mind—it was just that he liked to curse when he was climbing, it gave him a kind of a rhythm. They were both feeling a certain excitement at the possibility that the megafire was maybe now only wisps of white smoke, the last wheeze of a dying catastrophe. Jack wrapped a leg around the thinning trunk with the instinct of a rider on a bucking pony. He shielded his face with his forearms and shoved his head through a fragrant spray of needles and looked to the north-west. The happy curse that was halfway up his throat caught like a bone.

"What?" Wynn said, expecting a shout. "What?"

Silence.

"You okay?"

"Not really."

"What's wrong? You get sap in your eye?" But he knew what was wrong, he knew Jack well enough. "It's bad, huh?" he said.

"I don't know if bad is the word, Big. Give me a minute."

Jack said that sometimes. *Gimme a minute.* It was when he was about to take the stern paddle through a heavy rapid. He said it when he was overcome with emotion, and he'd said it in a brew pub in Lake Placid a few weeks ago when a very large summer person in a Ralph Lauren shirt had returned to the bar to find Jack talking to his wife. Jack hadn't known it was the man's wife, but he had unerring antennae for a-holes and they were vibrating strongly. The girl wasn't wearing any kind of a ring and she'd seemed quite eager to talk. But the man didn't have much of a sense of humor and Jack's antennae hummed. Jack stood, willing to move off and let it go, but the man had tapped his shoulder and said, "Hey, dude, you think you can just worm in when a guy goes to the pisser and worm off when he comes back?" Jack set his Red Canoe Lager down on the table and told the man to give him a minute. The man looked confused, because it was not rhetorical—Jack was actually trying to decide what to do; and then he made his decision and decked him. (Later in the car Wynn had said, laughing, "So much depends upon/a red/canoe/beaded with beer/sweat/ beside the white/dickhead.") So now when Jack said *Gimme a minute* Wynn felt his guts tighten.

Jack called down finally, "You ever feel like you're in a weird dream?"

"Like when we're hanging out?"

"You know, if you were up here you might not be cracking jokes."

"Bad?"

"Well." Jack hacked and spat down to the other side of the tree from Wynn, adjusted his footrest in the crotch of a limb. "The plume is rolling due south. Maybe a little east. Why—"

"Why we haven't smelled it."

"Yeah, and it's not really a plume, Big. I'd say you should climb up here but no point in two of us having nightmares."

"I guess."

"It's frigging clouds. Looks like a thunderhead. And it's a lot closer. Maybe a quarter, a third the distance of what we saw the other night. I can see the frigging flames. Like the leading edge under the smoke."

"How far do you think?"

Silence.

"Jack, how far?"

"I dunno. Maybe twenty miles."

Silence. Wynn said, "The other night we thought it was twenty-five or thirty. So it's come maybe five or ten miles in two days."

"Yeah, maybe."

"It's getting colder."

"Hold on."

He shinnied down, lowered himself limb to limb, and at the bottom branch he swung out away from the roots and dropped the last five feet to a bed of needles. "What'd you say?"

"I said it's getting colder. Maybe it'll slow."

"Yeah, maybe." Jack dusted bits of bark off the front of his shirt. He didn't sound convinced. He looked up at his friend. "I've seen a few wildfires, Wynn."

Wynn winced. Jack almost never called him by his given name. It meant shit was serious, like when his mother said, "Wynn

Peter Brelsford . . ." That was bad. He said, "You've seen a lot of fires *and* . . ."

"Right. Biggest fucker I've seen by far. Looks like a hay barn going up times a million."

"In eight or ten days the river will be wide. A hundred yards anyway. Maybe."

Jack raised an eyebrow and snagged the Skoal out of his shirt pocket and pried off the lid and offered it to Wynn, who shook his head. "That thing," Jack said. He took a large dip, tamped it into his lower lip. "Won't even notice. It'll jump the river like a semi running over a chipmunk."

"Yeah, but if we're in the middle of the river . . ."

Jack shrugged. "Maybe. The air gets superheated. That's what makes a firestorm. The rolling smoke is actually gas, and if the wind is right and it ignites, it'll flash-bake you a quarter mile away."

"It's getting colder, though, right?"

Jack huffed a breath. "But we don't want it to get colder, huh? I mean, for the whitewater. Or snow. That's funny, isn't it?"

"Nothing seems funny."

"I wonder what happened to those people."

~

They hiked back to the boat. They didn't talk as they zipped up and clipped the waist belts of their life vests. They were about to get on moving water. The vests were light, fitted lifejackets made for paddling. They hadn't worn them on the lakes except for the day of storm but now they did. Even in flat swift current a fast eddy turn could capsize a canoe. They were both thinking that in ten minutes the die would be cast. They'd shove the canoe into the current and head downriver, and the option of trying to find the couple, or whatever they were, and calling in a ride from their sat phone would be gone. Most everyone these days carried a phone. Except them. Except diehards nostalgic for the days of the voyageurs. Neither said a word. They'd made their decision, their nondecision; there was nothing else to do. They could try to paddle hard, harder than they ever had, and make longer days. And get to Wapahk as fast as they could. They could try to beat the fire.

Without a word Wynn went to the stern and found the cam straps and began lashing in the food and clothes barrels. He buckled in the extra lifejacket. Carrying one was required on certain rivers and it had become a habit. He ran a strap through the waterproof soft case of their rifle and snugged it tight, just ahead of the stern thwart, right side. He made sure the clips that opened the bag were easily accessible. He wasn't sure why. He just felt better knowing he could grab the gun fast.

They had brought the rifle to shoot caribou and to protect against bears near the bay. Nobody used to, but the warmer winters had changed everything. With the ice regime changing, the lean summer season for the polar bears was extended, and hungry bears in early fall were known to rove upriver looking for food, sometimes as far as fifty or sixty miles. Some were near starving and would eat anything that moved. There were also wolves and black bears, though neither Jack nor Wynn seriously thought of those as a problem. The unspoken reason for having a gun was that neither felt comfortable going for a long trip into the northern wilderness without one.

CHAPTER THREE

When Jack's mother died, Jack's father, Shane, stopped talking. It wasn't like Jack was missing much—his father had been a man of few words, unlike his father's brother, Lloyd, on the next ranch over, who could talk the bark off a tree. But later, over the years as his voice returned, Shane had told Jack stories about Uncle Lloyd, and whenever they were all together Jack could see how much his dad loved him. Shane told Jack that growing up he had not resented his older brother's volubility, he had admired it. They were Irish twins, eleven months apart, and Shane said he would often find himself in a circle of mutual friends listening to Lloyd tell a story he knew was wildly embellished. Lloyd might be recounting a ride through the Devil's Thumb lease with their cousin Zane, intoning, "Well, Zane, you know he's a gangly sonofabitch, shot up so fast in high school they had to climb halfway up his backside to find a place to hang his asshole." Laughter. "He was riding ahead of me on the trail, turned back and was trying to tell me some goddamn thing, and he hit the limb of this cottonwood and it knocked him out of the saddle. Well, you know he may not be that smart but he's quick as a snake in a boot and he grabbed that branch and he was hanging there squirming and I just rode on under and picked him up. There we were, riding together like newlyweds. He was half up on Shirley's neck and I squeezed him around the waist and said, 'Well, this is cozy. How's that saddle horn feel . . .'" Laughter.

Shane said it wasn't quite the way it had happened but it was somehow more true to the moment than if Lloyd had just told it dry, and it was way more fun. Jack did notice one thing, and it was something he loved about his uncle: Lloyd never embellished the bones of a hunting or fishing story. The fish never got bigger nor the rack of the bull elk wider. Inches, feet, miles, weather, were all surprisingly accurate. Shane said that Lloyd had once told him that a great storyteller had to know when never to lie. "Hunting and fishing's so much fun," he said, "only a pissant needs to lie about it." Jack could see that in all his father's dealings with Lloyd—splitting up the ranch after their parents died, sharing the lease, covering for each other in calving time, and coping with irrigation—Shane trusted his brother more than any other person on earth. Jack knew that Lloyd made life more fun, it was that simple, and without ever compromising the dead seriousness of it. That was a person to ride the river with.

Jack's father may have blamed himself and gone just about mute, but so did Jack—blame himself. That morning he had insisted on acting like a big man and taking up the rear. He'd never done it before. His gray, Duke, was much more athletic than sweet lumbering Mindy—if it had been him behind his father when BJ balked, Duke would have kept his footing. It was his fault for trying to be bigger than he was. His damn fault. In truth, at eleven he was already a constitutionally modest kid, and the accident just reinforced his aversion to drawing attention to himself or overreaching. He liked to be good at what he did—both his mother and father had instilled the value of that; there was nothing really more important other than treating animals and people with decency and respect— but not a lot of people had to know about it. What good did bragging do anyway? He had a few good friends who respected him and would do anything for him. Why did anyone else need to be impressed?

When he opened the envelope that said he'd gotten into Dartmouth, his father didn't hoot or take him out to a celebratory dinner at the Tabernash Tavern; he looked at him with an odd expression, half pride, half sorrow, and said simply, "Your mother would be over the moon." Over the moon. She was over the moon. It was almost exactly how he had been thinking of her these past years. When he walked halfway to the horse barn on a cold night and stood in the frozen yard and watched the moon climb over Sheep Mountain, he sometimes whispered, "Hi, Mom." He wasn't sure why, it just seemed that if she were to be anywhere it would be there. Maybe it was because his favorite book when he was very little was *Goodnight Moon*. She had read it to him over and over, and after she drowned he kept the battered copy on the little shelf above the bed and sometimes fingered the worn corners and flipped through it before he slept.

And it was books he took solace in. When he wasn't out on the ranch, or riding the lease, or fishing. He eschewed team sports—he felt like they were a bunch of kids showing off— and he kept most of his reading to himself. Not even his English teachers knew the depths of his growing erudition, but the school librarian did, as did Annie Bosworth down at the Granby Public Library. They knew. They also knew his instinctive modesty and shyness, so they encouraged him with guidance but never made a big deal of his extraordinary voracity, nor of his range. They simply kept him in books.

He and Wynn had that in common, a literary way of looking at the world. Or at least a love of books, poetry or fiction or expedition accounts. Wynn was a straight-up arts major who took a lot of courses in comparative literature, particularly French. Jack was engineering and supremely comfortable in the language of mathematics, but for the rest of his courses he took anything to do with poetry or novels, and he had especially adored American literature from the beginning. They had met even before the first day at school, on a freshman orientation trip, a four-day backpacking romp through the White Mountains. He and Wynn had rambled way out ahead of the group and talked nonstop, about canoes and rivers and climbing, but also about how Thoreau did his laundry across the pond at Emerson's house and how Faulkner was such a terrible drunk and womanizer and whether "Spring and All" was as good and important as "The Waste Land." Jack was startled. He'd never had conversations like this with another kid, and he'd never imagined anyone else his age would love to read as much as he did—especially a guy who seemed to be able to more than handle himself in the woods. They were best friends from that first day, and whatever else they were doing, they never went very long without trading books.

One thing they talked a lot about on that first hike was Louis L'Amour. Once they'd discovered they were both avid readers and had gotten over their shyness about it they began to reel off authors and books, what was good about them and bad, what they loved. It was a breathless conversation, and not only because they were hauling ass down the north side of Mount Madison. And then they were both relieved to find that the other was not at all a literary snob. The classics and the canon were one kind of animal, but sometimes a trashy yarn that ran headlong with no pretensions was just as good. Or at least as fun. And so they could admit that they'd both read probably every Louis L'Amour pulp western extant, even the ones that mysteriously appeared years after he died. Wynn read them because the aspen forests, the sage meadows, the sandrock canyons of the West were as exotic and enticing as anything he could imagine. And because the characters rode horseback through that landscape, and splashed across ice-rimed creeks, and pushed through herds of elk, and calmed their quivering horses when they picked up the scent of a lion or the blood trail of its kill. The heroes made camp in the ferns beside a stream spilling from snowcapped peaks and rubbed down their horses with halms of wheatgrass, and they kept their fires small and "smokeless" so they didn't alert their enemies. Jack read them because everything in them was familiar but shiny-familiar, not quite like the life he knew but the way things ought to be. Especially the part about killing all the bad guys and getting the girl.

They had been talking so much and hiking so fast and not even noticing the weight of their packs that they outstripped the group by a few miles. When they got to a stream they unbuckled the waist belts and slipped the backpacks off their shoulders and leaned them against the hemlocks. Wynn had a filter bottle so they filled it in the cold brook and drank and filled it again. "Look," said Wynn, "this is kinda refreshing." He reached down to the base of a balsam fir where the clover-like wood sorrel was covering the roots. He pulled up a handful and handed half to Jack and crumpled the bunch into his mouth. And puckered. Jack hesitated, then followed.

"Sour," he said.

"Kinda thirst-quenching."

"I guess."

They sat on a mossy boulder overlooking a low falls that spilled into a black pool infused with bubbles. Jack had never been in the mixed hardwoods of the East, but though they were alien, they felt comfortable to him, too. The rhythm of the ridges and streams was different, softer, less relief in the ups and downs, no rimrock, and more sheltered, too—the dense woods covered the valleys and went nearly to the tops of the mountains—but once he got used to the cadence, he liked it. A little claustrophobic, but he'd get used to it.

"Brookies in there, huh?" Jack said.

"If we had a bare hook we could probably catch them with a piece of our shirt. That plaid one of yours."

Jack laughed. "Hey, use your own goddamn shirt." He opened a Ziploc of nuts and raisins and M&Ms and handed it to Wynn, who said, "I hate people who eat all the M&Ms."

"That's what you wanna do, be my guest." They looked at each other and laughed.

And so they discovered that they were both fishermen, too. Check, check. They decided to make a small fire and boil water for tea. Why not? When the rest of the little group showed up they were stretched out by embers, sipping hot Lipton's from plastic cups. The trip leader, a junior, just shook his head. They got a reputation after that.

~

Now as they zipped their lifejackets and slid the canoe into the water and hopped in; as they paddled for the middle of the cove, which narrowed toward the north and began to show current and funneled into a wide *V* that picked up speed and slipped down between banks of spruce; and as they looked ahead and saw the horizon line of the first rapid and dug in and paddled hard for the right bank—as they truly began to run the river, they didn't think about anything but making it into the wide eddy pool along the right shore so they could scout the falls. But every river story they had ever read was just beneath the surface of their imaginations and must have fired them with extra energy and braced them, too, because at least half of those stories did not have happy endings.

CHAPTER FOUR

They rode the ramp of current down into a rippling of low waves and then the current smoothed and they were between low banks of tamarack and pine, with the white trunks of birch staggered through like markers or signals of who knew what. A fallen half-submerged log lay off the right shore and its black head bobbed in and out of the current like the nodding dead. Jack looked away. They stayed on the right side of the river out of an abundance of caution. The river had been run many times and was well described, but it was not run every year and no one in Pickle Lake had heard of anyone running it this summer. A must-make portage was maybe the most critical expedient they had to deal with, that and running the rapids without mishap. Sometimes the landing spots were small and right above the lip of a falls. Rivers could change a lot year to year, did change, and so a fallen tree blocking the eddy to one of those mandatory take-outs, or the erosion of a cut bank that wiped away a landing beach, had to be assessed well beforehand if possible. If not, they had to be on their toes with an emergency backup plan. Once on a river in Maine it had involved Jack jumping into the water with the painter rope of the canoe and grabbing for a snag against the bank. To keep them from going over a falls. A last-ditch and dumb move they never wanted to repeat.

It was already afternoon. Ranks of high clouds had sailed in from the north and were scattering the sunlight on the woods and the water. A pair of green-winged teals turned fast over the river and dropped sharply to the current and drifted ahead of them for a while. They caught sight of the bald eagle or its mate double-pumping its huge wings to land in the top of a dead tree. Wynn noticed that the smells were different now—it smelled like a river, like moving water, a colder, cleaner scent, and he pulled it into his lungs, from where it seemed to run through every capillary of his body, and he felt happy. Lake paddling was one thing, but it was good to be on a stream. It had always been that way for him: he'd string his favorite four-weight fly rod and step into a brook and feel the current pressing his knees and the rhythms, even the natural laws, of pedestrian life were suspended and he felt immediately uplifted. It had been that way since he was a child. Jack felt the excitement, too. After his mother died on the Encampment, he made himself fish again, and swim in current. It was hard at first but he did it, and after a while he could separate the one river from all the rest.

They knew that the lip of the falls and the trail for the portage began just after the sweep of a wide right-hand bend and they paddled easily around it and saw easily the flat gravel beach and the dark opening of the trail through willows and they paddled across the gentle eddy pool which turned them upstream and they stroked right up onto smooth stones.

~

It was already afternoon but they could huck the portage and make more miles, but for some reason neither of them was ready to leave the lakes behind. They would make camp. They each lugged a personal blue barrel of camping gear and clothes and another of food and cooking stuff to a clearing on a rock bluff overlooking the drop. Four small barrels. There was an old log cabin there, very small, built probably for hunting by a Cree, someone who came in by a boat with a motor from the string of lakes. A good place to camp for a few weeks. Except for the noise. The rapid was so loud they almost had to shout to be heard.

"Yo!" Jack called over the roar of the falls. "Just hearing that sonofabitch makes me need to pee." The thunder throbbed and thumped and if you listened closely you could parse out the rush of a ledge, the sluice beside it, and the crashing hydraulic beneath. A thousand violent sounds.

"Right?" Wynn said. "Wonder how we'll sleep. I can feel it in the ground."

"Fine, because we don't have to try to run the damn thing."

Maybe somebody could—run it. In a kayak. It was probably Class VI, a series of ledges with a massive amount of water pouring through. It looked like the North Sea in storm being spilled down a staircase. Maybe seventy feet top to bottom and ramped over an eighth of a mile. One rock island in the middle, the size of a rowboat, supported one gnarled and stunted spruce. The living fact of it trembling there in the middle of the mayhem only made the cataract more terrifying.

The sun broke through a reef of cloud and lit the falls, blazing the snowy whitewater and somehow sharpening the sounds, and Wynn thought it was beautiful, too. The way sheer rock ridges are beautiful, and avalanches.

There were blueberries. As the sunlight swept over the cabin it warmed the low groundcover around it and loosed the scent of the fruit and the tang of Labrador tea. The blueberries covered the clearing. And they were ripe. A fire might be coming and the frost might have landed early, but right now the country felt unbridled and wild, and bountiful, and mostly benign. The funk and low-grade fears of the morning had passed. They felt like themselves again.

They went back through willows and alders for the small dry-bag packs, the lifejackets and fishing rods, the gun. It was a short enough walk around the falls, maybe four hundred yards in all. They'd haul the canoe out and leave it where it was until morning. The Kevlar boat was light and it was just as easy for one of them to flip it up on his shoulders and carry it. Easier for one. The center thwart was wide and yoked for carrying. They made a pile of the four barrels and a dry bag on the bluff overlooking the rapid. And then they sat against the bag and just enjoyed the sun soaking them from over the woods across the river. It'd be gone in a minute, more clouds were coming. They noticed how instantaneously the afternoon cooled in the shadow, but for now they could sit with nothing to do but close their eyes and let the sun warm their eyelids. Probably four or five more hours before it dropped over the trees. In a few minutes they'd make camp and then pick enough blueberries to make pie. Their version of one, made in a frying pan with Bisquick and brown sugar.

"You wanna fish?" Wynn said without opening his eyes. "There was a good-size creek right above where we took out."

"Be good to have a pan fry tonight, huh? Brookies and blueberries." As soon as Jack said it, it sounded corny. "How come something so good just sounded so lame?"

"Professor Paulson said alliteration was dangerous if you don't know how to use it."

"Seems to me you could say that about anything. A frying pan or a car jack."

Wynn thought about it. "Paulson said there was a principle in aesthetics: the more you prettify something, the more you risk undermining its value. Its essential value."

"I don't know what that means." Jack tossed a pebble over the edge of the bluff. "Sounds like something a professor likes to say. I guess he means like plants that put all their energy into brilliant flowers and not the roots."

"I guess."

"So what if the value is already there? A strong and beautiful woman puts on makeup. So what?"

"Maybe if she puts on too much she could look cheap."

"But she's not cheap, is she? She's still who she is."

Wynn looked at his buddy. Jack had this way of questioning platitudes, dogma, authority. Jack thought most of his professors were zombies.

They lay back on the bag in the sun and didn't say anything. After a minute Jack said, "What's the dude's definition of danger anyway? When he said using alliteration can be dangerous."

"Yeah, right?" Wynn, eyes closed, felt around him until his palm lay on a small bed of warm moss. "It's like when they say this or that writer took a big risk," he said. "What are the consequences? He might have to hit delete on his laptop?"

"Ugh," Jack said. "Some of these dudes need to get out more." He sat up, looked over the edge of the short cliff. "Running this drop is a risk. Or paddling through that frigging fire." As soon as he said it, he wished he hadn't. The leading edge of the cloudbank covered the sun as if in sympathy and Jack felt the goosebumps running over his arms.

"Let's go get some dinner," Wynn said.

They roused. They shook off their lethargy and found the rod cases in the pile. They each put on a light fleece sweater and dug out their fishing kits: small waist-belt packs with tippet, a couple of fly boxes—dries and nymphs—Gink floatant, soft-weight and split-shot. Nippers and forceps. That was it. They both carried clip knives out of habit, in the pockets of their pants. They had serrated rescue knives, too, slotted into plastic sheaths on their life vests, but the clip knives were with them everywhere, all the time, and they could thumb them open in a split second with one hand. They practiced it, like gunfighters drawing a gun, and they did it so often, around the fire, scouting a route, that most of the time they didn't even know they were doing it. A good skill if somehow you got snagged and were being dragged by a rope behind a runaway horse or boat. Jack's father had taught him to carry one when he was still a kid; he, Shane, had once saved his own life with a flip knife when he'd gotten bucked off a green-broke Arab and his foot went through the stirrup. He was getting dragged and beaten to death and he'd managed to double himself and reach his foot and haul himself up with one hand and cut the leather.

The reverberation of the whitewater was less menacing now that they'd lived with it for half an hour and knew they could easily portage around it, and they walked back through the brush to the beach.

They unshucked the four-piece rods from their PVC tubes and pulled free the ribbons that tied them and unrolled the soft cloth sheaths. They slid out the slender sections. Jack had a Sage (green cloth), Wynn a Winston (red cloth). Wynn rubbed the butt end of each tapered piece against the side of his nose to lubricate it just a little before he twisted it into its hole, a trick his mother had taught him that kept the sections from locking up when you pulled them apart. He and Jack snugged together the pieces of the rods and slipped the reels into their saddles and tightened the lock rings. They ran the lines through the guides and checked their leaders.

They left the tubes in the canoe, and Jack held the end of the leader against the cork handle and reeled up the slack until the line lay taut against the rod. He began walking up the shore. The creek flowed in at the top of the beach. Like the one that ran through the last camp, it was slow and tea-colored with peat and tannin. And as they stepped slowly to the open bank they saw shadows darting. Brookies. Good.

They began to fish. Jack tied on a dark elk-hair caddis—he didn't think it would matter much what he threw—and crimped the barb with his forceps. Easier to lose a fish with no barb and they were fishing for dinner but he did it anyway. He moved upstream twenty yards to the beginning of the first big trees and into the sachet scent of the spruce. He began to cast into a slow pool. The pool was darkened by clumps of a fine dark grass that waved along the sandy bottom like hair. He made long casts into the deep shade of an undercut bank, and as soon as the fly touched water on the third cast he got a strike. The fish bent the tip of the rod hard and jerked it wildly and Jack laughed out loud because as he hauled it in he saw it was no bigger than the palm of his hand. Ounce for ounce a wicked fighter. He held it lightly in the shallow teawater at his feet and marveled at the intricate crinkled green patterns on the top of its head, and wondered again how natural selection could have scribed them. He slipped out the small hook easily. The trout wriggled wildly in his hand and darted free. "Go, go!" he whispered. He watched the little missile lose itself in the shadows of the grass. He almost always let the first one of the day go. It was respect.

Wynn waded into the shallows at the mouth. The river out of the lake already carried a load of silt from the banks and would be too murky to fly-fish, but the creek was clear and dark. If they were going to catch fish from now on, it would be in these side streams. He threw a tiny parachute Adams, a short cast into the middle of the barely moving brook, and instantly got a bump. He set the hook and threw the tiny brook trout airborne. It was not much bigger than a minnow. It landed in the water near his feet and he brought it in and cupped it gently and apologized and turned out the hook, and it shook itself as if waking from a bad dream and shot away.

They fished. They were both very good, but from a distance anyone could tell them apart. Not just that Wynn was bigger and heavier or stayed in the water wherever he could, but in their styles: Jack made his casts with an offhand grace, as if he were barely watching the line, he gathered it and stepped while taking in the wider circle of the banks, the woods, he cast with near indifference; the loop was always clean but sometimes low over the water and sidearm. If he false-cast he did it once to shake the water out of a dry fly, and the line lay straight and the fly landed lightly, always, as natural as a settling bug. If his wrist bent at the last moment to force the line upstream into a stiff wind, he didn't care. He fished almost as unconsciously as he walked or breathed. Wynn was different. He was more studied and he thought about everything. He calculated drift and knew before he threw the rhythm of the mends, and he divided the stream into quadrants, and if he was prospecting he worked across the slices of current, and if he was nymphing he worked one depth across, then dropped the fly a foot deeper into the column and worked back. He had learned from both parents and he had read a ton of books. His mother, Hansie, was an especially good fisher and teacher. His rod was almost always high, the metronome of the tip moving eleven to one on the clockface, or ten to two, the classic cast. His roll cast was textbook, and he double-hauled into the stiffest wind with the perfect cadence of a treadle. Jack sometimes watched his buddy fish and thought it was funny that he himself was the engineer and not Wynn. They caught about the same amount of fish.

Now they were having fun and laughing with the voracious brookies and letting every fish go. A pair of flycatchers chattered nearby and blew on thin reeds as they worked through the trees. The brookies were mostly tiny and they were crazy exuberant, like little kids. They darted for the fly and missed, or they were so excited they jumped right over it, or they bumped it and seemed to bounce off. Often two would try to hit it at once. Jack finally unshucked his Leatherman and snipped the hook right off the fly and tried to land the fish at the instant of strike. He managed to get a couple out of the water, but not for long. He heard a whistle.

He glanced downstream and Wynn was reeling in and motioning with his head to come down fast. It wasn't a fish—he was staring at the big river. Jack reeled in all his line and trotted down the stony bank. Wynn had stepped up onto dry land and he was staring dead upriver. Jack got to him and didn't say a word. He stood at his shoulder and they both peered upstream.

CHAPTER FIVE

They saw a boat. A canoe, green. It rounded the wide curve of the bend and came fully into view in the middle of the river. Not good. In another fifty yards whoever it was wouldn't have much time to make the beach for the portage on river right. They'd go over the falls.

"Shit, I wonder if they know," Wynn said.

"They're not giving themselves a whole hell of a lot of time."

Jack whistled, a searing ballpark jeer, and they both started waving their arms, motioning the paddlers to their side of the river. The flycatchers quit calling. And as the boys squinted they saw that it wasn't paddlers, not two—two with twice the power to move the boat—it was one. A man, hatless. They could barely see the figure, and the flash of the paddle in the patchy sunlight. A few strokes, then rest, heedless in the center of the relentless current.

They waved and whistled, both now. And they saw the paddle stop. And stop for more than a beat, two. It stopped as if frozen, stopped altogether in some surprised consideration.

"Yeah, that's right," Jack murmured, almost with scorn, "reconsider your line. Think about not committing suicide." He whistled again and Wynn's left forearm came up to protect his nearside ear. "Hey," Jack said. "Fuckin' A, that's just one dude."

Jack was going to loose another whistle and wave when they saw the paddle start to move again. It glinted sunlight and the sunlight passed, buried in cloud, and they felt the chill. Whoever it was began to dig. And then in a sign of an experienced canoeist he made a broad turn of the boat upstream and angled the bow toward the right shore and began to ferry across. Good. But what the fuck? That's what Jack thought. There should be two paddlers, a man and a woman.

Wynn was just glad to see that the man in the canoe had some sense and at least some basic skills, because it looked like he, too, was committing himself to run the river.

~

The man let the bow fall off and aimed for shore. He took a few hard strokes for speed and made a smooth swing across the eddy line. He ruddered on the left side so as not to turn straight upstream and he held his angle across the pool and let the bow grind up onto gravel. Good. They were both holding their rods, but they stepped forward in unison without a word and grabbed the man's bow, and together they pulled him up onto the beach so that only his stern stayed in water. Their eyes swept over the boat. It was a green Old Town Penobscot, heavy but tough. Well scratched and gouged. The man kneeled center thwart in solo paddler position, and they counted four dry bags, two forward, two aft. Just ahead of him on top of a bag, under a strap but in no case, was a plated Winchester Marine 12-gauge—a short-barreled shotgun. Jack knew what it was because he had one at home. The boys took it all in. They were more interested in the man's face. He was young, maybe midthirties. Mussed dark curly hair, a few days of beard, red-rimmed blue eyes, a stunned look, maybe panic or shock. The man did not thank them for the help in landing the boat. He did not speak. He looked from one to the other.

"Maia," he said. It was a croak. "Mai—" Like it was hooked in. The word. Hooked in like a half-swallowed fly.

Wynn said to the man gently, "Hold on. Why don't you come up? You can stand. You're on the beach."

The man didn't seem to understand. Jack murmured, "Maybe he's French or something. Or a Swede. The Europeans are crazy for these rivers."

"Yeah, maybe."

"I'm not a Swede," the man croaked. It was a half bark. And then his face crumpled. He began to cry. The boys stared. "My wife," he said finally. "She's missing. Gone."

~

They set their rods inside their own canoe and helped the man out of the boat. He wore a green plaid wool shirt, and knee-high gum boots as they did, and he staggered when he tried to stand on the stones. Jack caught him. "Hey, hey," Jack said. "What's wrong? What's wrong with your leg?"

Wynn looked down. The man's pants, the right thigh, were ripped and stained with blood. "Nothing," the man said. "I stumbled in the fog, it's nothing."

"That doesn't look like nothing. What'd you do, get speared by a deadfall?"

"It's a scratch." The man was almost vehement.

Jack let it go. "Whyn't you come up here and sit for a sec?"

The man looked at them as if for the first time. It was a feral look, almost wild with grief or fear. He turned back to the canoe and slid his shotgun out from under the strap and slung it over his shoulder. Jack glanced at Wynn and then led the limping man to a ledge of bedrock back of the beach. The granite made a high bench and Jack leaned him against it. Wynn had brought his filter water bottle up with him and he handed it to the man, who drank greedily.

"What do you mean, she's gone?" Jack said.

The man blinked. "Gone," he said. "The night the fog came in. When it cleared I saw another canoe. Far off." Jack noticed the man's right hand feeling shakily for the strap of the gun. "We—we've gotta get down. Get down and tell someone."

Wynn, even stooped, hands in pockets, towered over the man. It was the posture he took when he was concerned and didn't know what to do. Like he was trying to provide proximity and shade. When Jack saw him like that he always called him La Tree. Now La Tree looked dismayed. He didn't understand. Jack took the water bottle from the man's hand and gave it to his friend. "Refill this, will ya?" Wynn took it without a word and turned up to the creek. The water was clearer there and wouldn't clog the filter with sediment.

"Take a deep breath, dude," Jack said. "That's it, breathe. Whoa, don't cry. We'll figure this out." The man pressed his face into his sleeve. Jack put his hand on his shoulder. He said, "I need you to focus." It was a command.

The man's head came up. For a split second his blurry eyes were clear. And then they fogged over again. "Huh?" he said.

"I need you to focus," Jack said. "Something's not right. Now tell me what happened."

The man studied Jack. It was an assessment, a measuring. Jack also smelled fear. He shook his own head as if to clear it. Why did he feel so confused? The man didn't think that *they* had carried off his wife, did he? He was clearly in shock— something very bad had just happened.

Wynn returned and handed the man the full bottle and resumed the stooping tree pose. Jack said, "He's about to tell us."

Wynn said, "Maybe we should ask his name. What's your name?"

"Pierre."

"See? French," Jack murmured.

"Not French," said the man.

Wynn stared at his buddy. The man needed aid and succor—
why was he being a hardass?

"Tell us," Jack said.

The man seemed to draw back. He was looking at them as
if they had just asked for his wallet. In unison, out of some
unspoken courtesy, they both took a step backward. Pierre kept
his hand on the strap of the gun and blew out a long breath.
"We were camped," he said. "On the east shore. Not sure—a
few miles down the lake. It got cold. And then late the fog
came in. We'd never seen that. Before all the wind." He began
talking fast, in some kind of panic. "She said she had to go,
you know—"

"We know," Jack said, and Wynn glanced at him, puzzled. He
was never this impatient.

The man sucked at the water bottle. He wiped his eyes with his
forearm. "She unzipped the tent and went out into the fog and
I never saw her again."

Wynn started forward. *"What?"* he said.

"I never saw her again. There was a berm behind the camp. I
figured she went behind it. She took a flashlight. I found the

light but I never saw her. I looked for hours, calling and calling, but it was useless in the dark." His words ran fast, then jumbled into each other.

"And?" Jack said.

"I searched all day today and nothing." His head hung and he looked at his feet and his mouth began to quiver.

"Jesus," Wynn said. "Were there any tracks? Any sign?"

The man hung his head and shook it.

"No sign of a bear? There are plenty of black bear."

The man shook his head. "There was another canoe," he said. "Two men. We kept seeing them at a distance. I don't know . . .'"

"Yeah, we met them," Wynn said. "The two drunks. They were kind of creepy."

Jack was watching the man. He pushed his cap back and rubbed his forehead. He was trying to make sense of it. He said, "The night the fog came in. You mean the night before the morning of the fog or the night after?"

The man's head came up. Tears streamed on his sunburned cheeks and dripped off his lightly bearded chin. They fell to the dark stones and blackened them with drops like rain.

"What does it matter?" Wynn said.

"I can't think," the man said. "She's gone. Maia's *gone!*" It was almost a howl, of rage and grief. It rose over the rush of the falls and echoed off the wall of trees. It did not have the pure longing of a loon but it was just as loud.

Wynn put his hand on the man's shoulder. "Just sit for a second—we've gotta think."

"There's nothing to think about," the man shot back. He wiped his face on his sleeve. "We've got to get to the village."

"Do you have a satellite phone?" Wynn said.

"No."

"Were you two gonna get picked up on the lake?"

"No."

"You were planning to paddle down to Wapahk?"

"Yes."

"So no one's coming?"

"No."

"Even if we sprinted to the village—that'd take ten days. At least."

The man's eyes glassed over again. It looked like he was drifting back into shock. Wynn breathed and tamped down a rising desperation. He turned to Jack. Jack was watching the man, puzzled. Wynn shivered.

"We're gonna go look," Wynn whispered. Not soft enough that the man didn't hear, and Pierre started forward as if burned.

"What?" he said.

"Jack and I are going to portage back to the lake and go look for her. The currrent's too strong to paddle back up, so we'll carry the canoe."

"We are?" Jack said. He looked at his buddy with a burnished admiration.

Wynn straightened. "If we don't, who else will?"

"Hell yeah," Jack said. He pulled down his cap brim. "That's exactly what we're gonna do."

"You can't do that," the man said. "It's *up*stream. Probably a couple of miles. There's no *trail.*"

"Doesn't matter," Jack said. "We're young and strong." He said it like a warning.

~

Jack held his arm straight out and lifted it to the partially obscured sun. He cupped his hand and counted down hand's-widths to the treetops across the river. Each finger was fifteen minutes, the hand held out without the thumb an hour. His father had taught it to him. "We've got over four hours of day-light," he said. The man stared at him.

"What does she look like?" Jack said.

The man blinked. He couldn't digest what was going on. He said, "Look like? She's—I don't know. My height. Long brown hair. Greenish eyes. I mean, Christ, if there's a woman alone—"

"Hold on," Jack said. "Stay put." He glanced at Wynn. "Can you keep him company?" He trotted down the trail toward the cabin. When he came back five minutes later he was carrying their fleece sweaters and raincoats, the day pack with survival gear, and a half-full dry bag with shoulder straps. Also their life vests, along with the spare. Slung over his shoulder was the Savage .308.

~

"Bring the fishing rods and your water bottle," Jack said to Wynn.

"The rods? Are we gonna fish?"

Jack shot a look at his friend. "What if we get caught out?"

"Okay," Wynn said. "Good thinking." He went to the canoe and lifted out the rods. Jack began stuffing the dry pack with the survival box and the extra clothes, the spare life vest. He rolled the seal top and clipped it. "You take this," he said to Wynn and handed him the pack. "I'll take the canoe first."

Wynn had seen his buddy go into command mode a few times, but it had always been in an emergency—when one of their NOLS teams was caught in a lightning storm on a ridge above treeline; when late-winter weather had blown in on the Dolores and a raft had flipped just before dusk. Was this an emergency? Definitely. The man had lost his wife. So if Jack seemed brusque, there was a reason.

The man, Pierre, was watching them. It was as if he couldn't keep up with everything that was happening. Wynn supposed he was in shock. The man pushed himself up off the rock ledge. "Hey," he said. He winced as he weighted his right leg. "You better take this." He limped to his boat and opened a small clear waterproof bag clipped to a thwart. He pulled out a walkie-talkie handset. It was a Midland 36-Mile with a camo pattern. Jack recognized it; it was the same model he and his dad used at home, riding and hunting. In rough country it didn't go thirty-six miles but it was usually good for fifteen. The man handed it to Wynn. He said, "Maybe you could . . . tell me . . ." Wynn grimaced. It looked like the man would break down again. But he didn't. "Maybe you could keep me posted," he said. "It should have a full charge."

"Yeah, sure." Wynn clipped the handset to his belt. He hoisted the dry pack, picked up the fishing rods. Jack was clipping their life vests around the two seats. As long as there was one on each end they wouldn't unbalance the canoe. He put his arms through the extra one for padding. Jack squatted and lifted and heaved the upturned canoe onto his shoulders. Piece of cake. The nineteen-footer was made of ultralight Kevlar and weighed forty-seven pounds. He could carry it all day. He nodded at Wynn, *Let's go,* and didn't look back at the man but began walking easily to the top of the beach.

~

They moved fast at the beginning. The going was easier than they'd thought. Jack had remembered to snap the map case to the bow and he had double-checked the distance: just over a mile and a half. Nothing on the topo but the hump of the moraine. They pushed themselves.

At the speed they were walking they could get to the lake in less than an hour. It was easy going at first, open under the mixed woods along the shore, the underbrush light in the shade of the old trees, only a few spots where Jack had to drop the canoe and drag it through a thicket of willows or spruce limbs. He got scratched up, but who cared. Where they could, they swung out into the open along the riverbank. The willows and alders were denser here, but Jack thought how it was the same as the creeks back home: the animals clearly preferred the river's edge. A good game trail cut through most of it. They saw bear scat crumbled with the seeds of berries, and moose tracks bedded into the deeper moss. The pack was heavier than Wynn thought it should be, but compared to many packs he'd carried it was featherweight. Then they got to the tail of the moraine and they had to hump over it. It was steep and in places eroded to rock and Jack climbed slowly, swinging the bow between branches, threading trees, and stepping up hard to shove the upside-down boat through the limbs of the firs. Wynn could hear him breathing, but they didn't speak. Wynn wondered if it was like this for the biggest moose every day, trying to maneuver the broad antlers through mixed timber. At the steepest spots he put a hand on the swinging stern and spotted it, helping guide and push the swaying boat where he could, but the third or fourth time it unbalanced Jack as he stepped up on a root and he cursed hard and almost toppled.

"Jesus, Wynn, cut it out! I got this."

"Sorry."

Jack never spoke to him so sharply.

The other side had a more gentle slope, and where the moss and stones were wet Jack edged down sideways, and then they were on a grassy beach at the shore of the lake. The fleets of cloud had thickened rank on rank and it was now an almost unbroken overcast to the far horizon. It was a long lake, maybe nine miles. The water was slate-gray under a northerly wind and the waves pushed away to the farthest shore. Nothing on the water, nothing moving along the relentless wall of woods. No sign of a bird. It was desolate and leaden.

Paddling south would be easy with the wind at their backs. If the wind kept up and they got into a longer reach, the paddle back north would be a bitch. Every wave would spray up into their faces and lap the gunwales. Jack squatted and Wynn helped him flip the boat to the beach. They tugged off their sweaters and Jack unkinked his back. It felt like they'd almost run the distance. They should have: the sun was a third of the way to the trees.

Wynn handed his friend the water bottle and Jack squeezed it and drank the whole thing. "Thanks."

Wynn walked to the water and refilled it and drank. He thought how here, in the lee of the trees, the water was almost slick with calm, how the waves didn't start for over a hundred yards out.

Jack seemed ornery and edgy. Well. There was a lot to be edgy about, he guessed. He filled the bottle again and walked back.

"Something bad happened," Jack said.

"Whadda you mean?"

"I don't know what I mean."

"Well, there's a woman missing. Up here. That's bad. Really bad." Wynn offered the bottle again and Jack held up a hand. Wynn said, "He's certainly rattled. He just lost his wife. Also, he's injured. I should've taken a look at it." Why hadn't he? "When were we going to tell him about the fire? God," Wynn said. "Gimme a chew." Jack handed him the tin. Wynn said, "I've been thinking about those two dickheads on the island."

"Me, too."

"That trolling motor was heavy. They can haul ass. Way faster than paddling. I guess they could have caught up to them."

"Yeah." Jack said it, but he wasn't sure what he meant. He wasn't sure of anything. He turned to Wynn. "Let's get the fuck out of here before we get caught out." He meant caught out by nightfall. They shoved the boat in the water and picked up the paddles and lay in along the eastern shore.

~

They paddled hard, and with the wind they were at their previous camp in less than an hour. They could see their fire ring.

Jack was in the stern, steering. He brought them in close. They paddled by it and surfed the small waves downwind. A wave would pick them up and tip them forward and they'd gather speed and it would pass under; in the trough they'd wallow and it felt like they'd stopped dead but they hadn't. They paddled another half mile of thick woods to another tributary creek; they could see it running shallow through the sandbanks of its own deposits and over the cobbles of the beach. A berm like a dune covered in fireweed lay behind it.

"It's near here," Jack said. "Where we heard them. This feels like it could have been the camp."

Wynn shrugged. "Okay." Jack steered them to the shore and Wynn hopped out in the shallows and pulled the bow of the boat onto gravel. They walked inland. High on the beach there was another fire pit, remnants of char, who knew how old. They glanced at each other. Jack lifted his chin and called: *"Anybody here? Hey! Hey!"*

Wynn bent to the sand between stones and picked up a hair-clip, a blue metal barrette. He held it up. "No telling when, right?"

Jack didn't answer. He called again. Nothing. They walked south over the cobbles of the shore until they hit the creek. There were no other signs. Wynn called now, then Jack, and their shouts were carried away on the wind. They waded across the stream and lifted their voices, but when they got to a spur of dense woods their cries hit the wall of trees and died. The forest absorbed them. Nobody would make camp in the woods when there was an open beach and a creek nearby. They turned around.

After they crossed the stream again, they stood at a loss, look-ing out over the choppy water. Whatever they were going to do now, they'd better get after it: the sun had dropped and the whitecaps flecked more brightly in the long light of late after-noon and the air had chilled. Instinctively they moved inland toward the trees backing the beach and separated, each taking a different line. They'd search this spot that had at one time been someone's camp, and then they'd hop back in the boat and head a little farther down the shore.

"Jack!" Wynn yelled, and he was running. Wynn had been a hockey star at Putney. For such a lanky tree he could haul ass. He was running up the beach, angling for the berm, and Jack saw what he was aiming for. The tall fireweed at the top of the rise was moving. It shook and stopped and moved again.

CHAPTER SIX

A person crawled in the weeds. A woman on her right side, stretching and bunching like a broken caterpillar. She had lost blood. Her head was oozing over the left temple. Her face was a mask. The blood had dried and cracked. She crawled in the tall pink flowers and her rain jacket was open and her down vest was soaked in dried blood and covered in bits of dirt and moss. The blood was almost black and the fireweed blossoms trembled against it. Her eyes were half open and swollen and her mouth worked but uttered no sound. Wynn's first thought was, *Jesus, a bear. She surprised a bear in the fog.* He got to her first and his hands went right to her head. She jerked and writhed away. A whimper came from her throat and she tried to curl up. One arm went to protect her face.

Wynn had a hand on her shoulder and he was talking fast, saying, "Whoa, whoa! You're okay, you're okay! We've got you now, you're all right, please don't move, don't, hold still, hold still." The struggling subsided and she lay curled. "I'm Wynn, this is Jack. We're here to get you out of here." Wynn put his hands gently to her head and neck and kept talking, and it took a minute for the words to register, but she began to emit what sounded like sobs and her arm relaxed. Wynn glanced at Jack. He said softly, "Hey, we're gonna roll you over, make sure your back's okay. We're gonna get you out of here." It seemed to him she was listening. Her body went limp and he nodded to Jack and Jack went to her hips, and Wynn nodded again. "Ready?" "Yep." "Okay, three, two, one . . ." And they rolled her. Ever so gently they turned her together full on her back and laid her on the sandy loam at the top of the berm.

She was covered and stained with dirt and lichen. Her mouth was working. "Okay, hold still." Jack got his sweater off and Wynn pillowed it under the hollow of her neck. "Water bottle," he said to Jack. Jack ran. Wynn reached a hand to the side of her throat and pressed gently. Thready pulse and fast. Shock. Hypothermia. Lucky she survived the night. He reached for his clip knife and thumbed it open and cut into his left sleeve at the elbow. He slashed it as best he could and ripped it free. When Jack came back with the bottle he doused the sleeve and began patting away the oozing blood at the side of her head. And then she began to moan. The boys glanced at each other and Wynn said, "Clean that up very gently."

He reached for his belt and lifted the handset and keyed the mike, and said, "*Pierre? Pierre? We found her! She's alive but—*" and she moved, lurched beneath them, and then he heard Jack hiss, "*Fuck!*" and Wynn felt the sting of his backhand and the walkie-talkie went flying onto the stones below.

~

Stunned. He turned to Jack, who still had a hand on her head, trying to calm her. But Jack was looking at the walkie-talkie shattered on the rocks. As if he himself couldn't believe he had knocked it there.

"Sorry," Jack muttered. "Fuck."

"What?" Wynn blinked. "What was that? I was just telling him—"

Jack held up a hand. He was shaking his head as if to clear it. "We don't know, but now *he* does."

"We don't know *what*?" Wynn said.

"What if *he* did this, Big? What if it was him who tried to kill her?" Jack was trying to keep his voice low. Wynn stared. Jack said, "I've been thinking about it the whole way back here. While we were carrying up, paddling. Pierre said he lost her the night the fog came in. Bullshit."

Wynn looked over his shoulder back at the woods as if someone might be listening. "What?"

Jack whispered fast. "We heard them on the beach. Arguing, remember? They were shouting at each other. In the *fog*. You heard it."

Wynn had never seen Jack so agitated. "He said he lost her the night of the fog. Maybe he meant the night after."

"That's not what he said. I asked him that, remember? To clarify, and he backed off."

"Well."

"I'm telling you, the guy was lying from the start. I got that hit, I should've paid attention." Jack looked down at the blood-soaked rag in his hand, blinked. He blew out. "I mean, okay, we can't be sure of anything, but if he was the one who did this, now he *knows* we found her and she's alive."

~

None of that made sense. Wynn didn't speak after that. While Jack cleaned her up Wynn did his first-responder assessment, working from the head down. She had bruises on her abdomen. Her left shoulder appeared to be dislocated. They'd have to get to that. Full sensation and movement in fingers and toes. Her back, thank God, seemed to be okay. There was old vomit on her rain jacket, probably from the convulsions and nausea of a concussion. She drifted in and out of consciousness. They needed to get her stable. She was mostly soaked and had gone past shivering. She needed heat, liquids, rest, right now.

Now Wynn understood why Jack had been so testy, why he'd insisted on taking the fishing rods, the survival pack, the rifle. In case. In case they found just what they'd found. Still. The man had clearly been injured and upset, almost in shock. Some accident had happened, Wynn just wasn't sure what, and the man Pierre had missed her in the fog somehow. There were a dozen possibilities. Bear attack. Mother moose. The woman could have gotten lost in the fog in the woods and climbed a tree to locate the lake and fallen, cracked her head on a rock. Or: the two drunks. Not the most savory of dudes. They could have spotted the couple's canoe from a distance and stalked them. Seen their camp before the fog rolled in. Creepy. He shook it off.

He cleaned up her head. She began shaking hard. That was good in a way. They didn't have much first aid. They traveled light in that regard—they were boys. Sometimes on climbing trips they took a small bottle of iodine, some SecondSkin glue, and a partial roll of duct tape. Now in the emergency box they had a couple of packs of gauze, one bandage, the iodine, duct tape, Neosporin. They cleaned her head the best they could; it was a diagonal gash to the skull but not deep, maybe three inches long.

They needed to get her warm right away.

"Make a fire," Wynn said. Jack nodded. They had to warm her up, her core. They had bouillon cubes in the survival box and a few packets of ramen. They'd get her close to the fire and wrap her in the emergency blankets and whatever else they had and feed her hot liquids until the shaking stopped.

Jack shoved away through the tall weeds and Wynn doused the cut with iodine. She was half conscious. He washed the blood off her face. No more cuts, good. She was maybe watching his face, her eyes were slits, they blinked and she moaned. He found a needle and stout thread in the box, he'd packed it for gear repairs but knew it would work as backup for sutures, and he sewed up the cut where she lay. Her body shook in waves and she groaned, but he knew that with the dislocation and the crack to her skull the other pain would mostly mask it. Relative anesthesia. He shivered. "Done," he said. He patted it with gauze and bound the gauze to her head with the bandage.

Wynn glanced up at the sky: a solid overcast now, moving fast south. Fuck. He prayed it wouldn't rain. Well, if it didn't, the clouds could work for them and hold off the frost. He didn't think they'd move tonight—she wouldn't be ready, they'd have to camp here. The two emergency blankets were waterproof and they'd cover her, and he and Jack would keep the fire going and do the best they could. He held her head while she shook and he didn't turn but he could hear the crack and pop of the fire. For the first time Wynn looked at her. Not at the sum of her injuries but as a person lying in the weeds beside him. She was maybe early thirties, dark hair in a braid, hazel eyes, what he could see of them. She was lean, and she had even teeth, unbroken. A strong jaw, also in place, strong dark eyebrows. She looked tough. She must have been tough to survive the two days exposed. If they could get her through this part and she had no severe internal injuries, she would make it. What Wynn told himself. When the danger of hypothermia had passed he would have to reset her shoulder.

The fire cracked and popped and hissed, and when the wind eddied back toward the woods he could smell the smoke and it smelled like life. Maybe the first time he'd ever thought that. Jack was beside him, and Wynn said, "I don't think anything's fucked with her spine. Just in case, we'll carry her together." He didn't have to tell him that he'd take her head and shoulders and Jack would support her hips. "On three." They carried her. They could feel the shudders moving through her and they laid her on a Therm-a-Rest inflatable sleeping pad on a bed of sand Jack had cleared and smoothed by the fire.

Therm-a-Rest? It was green, Jack's. Wynn glanced at him.

"I got yours, too. And the tent."

"Damn." Wynn almost laughed but it came up like a cough. "No wonder the pack was so heavy."

Jack stuck his arm in the blue dry bag and pulled out the nylon cylinder of a stuff sack. A sleeping bag.

"Holy shit," Wynn said. "You brought the whole camp." In the bottom he felt both their bear sprays. Whoa. Wave of relief. Their sleeping bags were light, but they were water-resistant down. The fire was hot, they kept the woman back a couple of feet. They stripped off her wet pants and underwear and her rain jacket and wet sweater but her wool undershirt had wicked dry as she'd lost heat and they left it on. They wrapped her with the sleeping bags but left the side facing the fire open so that the heat could get inside her bed. Jack had pushed smooth stones into the flames so they'd heat up in the glowing embers, and when they were hot they'd let them cool to warm and use them like hot pads. He'd also thrown the one battered pot in the bag, and he trotted down over the cobbles to the lake and filled it with lakewater and set it on two rocks by the flames.

They squatted beside her and waited for the water to boil.

"You knew it'd be like this," Wynn murmured.

"I didn't know. Still don't. What happened. But I know the dude was lying. And thinking about it now, he did *not* want us to come back up here. He only gave us the walkie-talkie so he'd know if we found her." He raked coals under the pot. "Sorry about that part," he said again. He meant slapping the radio out of Wynn's hand. He'd never done anything like that.

"That's all right."

They felt the fire heat their knees, pants almost burning to the touch, and they scooched back. Wynn reached down and felt the nylon on the outside of her sleeping bag to make sure it wasn't too hot.

"Her shoulder's out," Wynn said. "I'm going to have to put it back in. When she warms up."

"You done it before?"

"No. I know the theory."

"I have. I did it for Pop once. I'll do it."

"Okay."

"I never heard Pop mewl, before or since, but he cried."

"Ouch. Okay. I'll explain it to her."

~

When the sun went down, so did the wind. They raked the stones out of the fire and let them cool to an even heat and wrapped them in their shirts and placed them in the sleeping bags with the woman. Pot, spoon, their two cups. What Jack had brought. He'd had a gut feeling they might be spending a night or two out. When her shaking stopped they stirred a bouillon cube into half a cup of water and blew on it until it wouldn't burn her and then they both propped her up and let her sip the salty liquid. She seemed awake enough to understand. Wynn thought she might have been badly concussed. They'd have to see. They let her drink the clear soup slowly and then Jack made up a cup of sugar water, not tea—no caffeine in case of a bad concussion. She drank that, too. She whimpered a little as she sipped but was otherwise quiet.

When she finished, Wynn said gently, "We're going to have to put your left shoulder back in. It's dislocated. Once we get it back in the socket you'll have a ton of relief." She blinked. "It's going to hurt a lot," Wynn said. "But just for a minute."

Her head may have moved up and down. Jack had thrown in their wool hats for good measure, and Wynn took his Ivy Darrow hand-knitted Putney ski hat and spread it open and worked it over her head and bandage. "Ready?"

Her eyes closed. Maybe that was an affirmative. Wynn had seen it before: injured people who had barely enough energy to shift a little, to eat, but not enough to talk. Strange that words took so much life force. She was half sitting propped back against him. Jack ran his hands up and around her left arm in its thin wool shirt. He felt up to her shoulder and he gently rotated the arm inward to its normal position and then pulled. Gently at first, then more firmly, then hard. She cried out, a peal of pain stronger and louder than they could have imagined, and then she was gasping and tears were running down her bruised cheeks and then she passed out. They laid her back down and zipped up the bags and let her sleep.

CHAPTER SEVEN

They stoked the fire all night. There was plenty of driftwood wracked on the shore. It didn't rain and the cloud cover kept the night warmer and it didn't frost. Jack set up the ultra-light tent, a tapered tube with an arched pole at either end that staked out taut, front and back. He snapped on the waterproof fly to cover it, as much for a little more warmth as anything, and they took turns stretching out and sleeping on Wynn's pad inside it. In a sweater and rain jacket and wrapped in one of the emergency blankets, they were cold, but it was doable.

It didn't rain. The low clouds lidded the sky and the wind dropped. Except for the flames of the fire, which sent their sparks toward the wall of trees and then shifted and blew out over the water, there was no light. Wynn stared across the lake westward and at times he thought he might have seen the faintest glow reflected in the overcast, but he would blink and it would be gone. He thought the distant fire was like a war zone, like a front in some battle that was too distant to hear but that would in a matter of days change your life forever. How it felt. The night was pitch, but Wynn could feel that the sky was moving overhead, scraping the treetops.

She must have slept. They'd gotten some ramen in her after dark and in themselves, too. Wynn carried a larger stone to the fire and sat beside her head. He covered it as much as he could with the hood of one of the sleeping bags, but he could see in the fluttering light the top of his ski hat, blue with a broad red band. Knit by his friend Pete's grandmother. The Darrows had the orchard one ridge over from his place, and he knew the hillsides blind from years of running through them in every season, from swimming in the pond at the lower edge. His favorite time was early May, when the slopes were a sea of white apple blossoms that perfumed the air with a scent so delicate and sweet he thought it might be the most enchanting smell on earth. Autumn, too, in the fields and woods, mid-October, the earth smells of fallen leaves slick with rain, of tall grasses and stony trails wet with cold rain and the cold stone smells of the brooks surging with the rush of all-night down-pours. That smell was unbeatable.

Why was he thinking of home? Because he wanted to be there, right now. This trip they'd looked forward to all year had taken a turn. That was okay. That's what adventures were all about: dealing with unforeseen dangers. And when you were with a friend as solid as Jack, there might be nothing better. But this was different. He sat in the wavering heat and felt the low sky raking overhead just beyond the firelight and he smelled rain. He hoped it held off. He hoped the sense he had of things slipping toward disaster would blow away like the clouds.

Right now he wanted to be home. He and Jack could both be there for a couple of weeks, end of summer, helping his dad put up firewood. Tonight, by now, Jess and his mom and dad would've gone to sleep. A northeast wind that presaged fall would be buffeting the windows, and he and Jack would sit by the woodstove with one lamp lit and talk about the canoe expeditions they would take. They'd step outside for air and if the wind was right they'd smell the apples ripening on the trees in the dark down the ridge. Funny to think that now, now that he was *on* the canoe trip they'd wanted to take the most.

This one. It had started like magic. The clear warm weather, the cool nights and stars, no northern lights yet, but they'd only been out a week. The fishing that seemed like cheating. They'd paddle to the edge of a lake, or into the mouth of a slough or creek and they'd throw dry flies and catch lake trout out of a dream. They'd throw big tufty Stimmies and tiny black gnats. Didn't seem to matter much. They'd barely touched their dried food and they were almost getting sick of pan-fried fish. They picked blueberries and raspberries and blackberries along the shores and they gorged themselves. Their mouths turned blue and purple and they laughed about how they could pick for an hour and never fill up a pot or a baseball cap. They ate them all. They were strong paddlers and made easy time across the lakes, and they challenged themselves to try to make the longest portages in one carry and they never could. Not with the rifle and fly rods and small barrels of food and gear.

The rifle. Wynn huffed out a breath. What had been the best trip ever was now ... what? It still seemed like a dream, but turning bad. He didn't think she'd been mauled by a bear, but it was possible.

He wished he had his pipe. It was anachronistic and on a wilderness trip there was nothing he enjoyed more—to stuff it with a vanilla burley blend and smoke it late by the fire. But he'd left it in camp. It had been his grandfather's, his father's father's. Whom Wynn had adored because he was a risk-taker and a goofball. The old old man, Charlie, had trained as a lawyer and married a Boston Brahmin and had worked on Wall Street for a few years and hated it; he'd moved to southern Vermont and become a respected amateur painter and early organic gardener and local historian. He painted barns and fields, but he also painted nudes, and the story went that he had two model mistresses, one widow and one widow aspirant, who'd told her drunk husband that if he made a peep she'd slit his throat the next time he passed out, which would probably be tomorrow. Charlie's youngest son, Wynn's dad, had inherited his father's fluid, honest line and sense of color but had eschewed fine art for the more practical pursuit of architecture. After college he had spent a year in Japan studying landscape and had never gotten over it, and he now built Japanese-inspired houses all over southern Vermont. The goofy, risk-taking fine-arts gene had skipped a generation and landed on Wynn. Who thought he'd be perfectly willing to spend half the year as a low-paid outdoor instructor if he could spend the other half living in some barn constructing art installations and sculptures.

He pushed the stub ends of driftwood into the embers and held out his right hand and heated his palm. Then he reached down and worked his hand into the sleeping bag wrapping her head, into the warmth of it. Warmth, good. Her core temp had come up, little by little, and the shivering and whimpering had stopped, and they kept putting warm stones in with her and retrieving them when they cooled. She had drunk a full cup of ramen and eaten a chocolate bar and now she was generating her own heat. He worked his fingers down and felt the pulse at her throat and it was steady and strong. Good. The shock, the worst of it, was over. The challenge would be to keep her out of it.

He turned his eyes away from the fire and out to the lake. The circle of light wavered over the stones of the beach. It flared in the wind and dimmed when the gust passed. The night was dense. The firelight could not penetrate to the water. Out there, in the felted blackness, was only sound. The lap of small waves, the sift of water sliding over water. He thought he heard a slap, he could have—the tail of a beaver? He glanced down beside him: the Savage .308 was there, out of its scabbard, scoped and chambered. When they had finished the portage Jack had unshouldered the canoe and reached for the gun on Wynn's shoulder. He'd thumbed the safety and levered the action and dug in his pocket for a single cartridge and shoved it into the top of the magazine and snapped up the lever. Now with the five in the magazine there'd be six shots. Tonight, in low voices, they had decided to leave the gun with whomever was on watch. No telling what the crazy fuckers on the island would do.

Maybe, Wynn thought, they were overreacting. Maybe she *had* been attacked by a bear. It had been his initial assumption. But the more he thought about her injuries, the more of a stretch it seemed. A bear clawed and bit and tore, it didn't club and punch and twist arms from their sockets. But a fall could have. If she'd tried to climb a tree as they had, a fall could have done it. Wynn shivered. He was now downwind of the flames, the smoke stinging his eyes, the heat billowing into knees and face; he wasn't shivering from cold. He realized that sometime in his musing he had reached for a chunk of driftwood and still held it. Damn, he must be getting sleepy. He reached out and laid it on the flames.

~

He got up and stretched and went to the woodpile and picked up an entire armload and fed it to the fire. They had scavenged the shoreline and stacked a pile of driftwood waist high. Might as well stay warm. And the way the megafire looked to be running, in a week or so all of this wood might be burned up anyway. He sat back down. He couldn't keep his eyes open. The day seemed interminable, it defied natural law, no day could last this long. He made himself stay awake and in what seemed like twenty minutes he woke up Jack and passed out in the tent.

CHAPTER EIGHT

They had oatmeal in the box, and brown sugar and tea. They boiled the oats and added sugar until it was sweet and spooned it into her. They made tea for themselves, ate a little after she did, let her drink hot sweet water. She sat up in the sleeping bags. She didn't say anything, but when Wynn held the spoon to her mouth she opened it, slowly—half opened it; it seemed her jaw was sore from whatever blows had blackened her eyes. She blinked when it was too hot or she'd had enough. She could use only one hand, but even that she barely had the energy to lift. The other arm they'd slung with two tied-together bandannas. When she had drunk most of the cup of hot water she half opened her mouth and emitted a rasping croak.

"What?" Wynn said, leaning his ear down close. "What'd you say? We?"

"She has to pee," Jack said.

"Oh."

She nodded, barely.

"Oh, okay."

They took up their now regular positions and Wynn held her under her head and upper back and Jack lifted her hips and knees and they carried her fifteen feet from the fire and set her down over a larger stone and let her half sit. They still held her torso. She was very weak.

"Can you pee like that?" Wynn asked. She was naked from the waist down from where they'd stripped off her wet clothes. She nodded. She did. They both felt relief as they heard it hitting the stones, almost as if it were they themselves emptying. When she finished, everyone held position for an awkward minute.

"Ipe," she whispered.

"Wipe? Oh, wipe! Got it!" Wynn said, a little too loud. This was all new territory for him. Jack, who had grown up on a ranch, held little stigma for bodily functions and no patience for squeamishness, said, "Just a sec," and ran up to the berm and yanked out halms of dried grass and brought them back. He handed them to her and she tried to take them but she was too weak. Her eyes spilled tears then. The tears ran unhindered down over her bruised cheeks and dripped off her chin.

"Okay, okay," Jack said gently. "I got this. Okay?"

She nodded faintly. He patted her with a bunch of grass and they carried her back. She was very weak. Her underwear and pants had been hanging by the fire and were dry, and Jack and Wynn worked one, then the other up her legs and snapped and zipped the fly and buckled the webbing belt. They worked her right arm through the sleeve of her zip-up fleece sweater and then through the sleeve of the rain jacket and zipped them up over her slung left arm. The wind had died, thank God. A light northwest breeze and the overcast had broken up. Just high clouds drifting slowly and bruised-rose underneath from the rising sun, which had not yet cleared the trees. No frost. They worked her dried wool socks over her feet and put her Gore-Tex hiking boots back on and laced them up. They doused the embers of their fire with lakewater. After the first hiss and the exploding puff of ash and steam and the sharp stench of char, they walked away from it and could smell woodsmoke. The first time in two days, and they knew again that they were keeping company with the forest fire.

~

They wrapped her in one of the sleeping bags and folded the emergency blankets, struck the tent, rolled up the ground pads, and packed their meager provisions in the canoe. Well, now there was room for her. They didn't even know her name. The man, Pierre, had said something like Maia, hadn't he? They set her in the middle, propped back against the dry bag. Wynn walked up the beach to retrieve the pieces of the walkie-talkie, he wasn't sure why. Maybe the guts of it were still good, maybe there was another party ahead of them on the river that had one, though he thought the odds were low. But when he got to the handset the plastic body was badly shattered. He tried the volume and squelch knobs, but nothing—it was dead. He scooped it up for the garbage bucket when they got to their gear. They shoved off. Wynn took the stern and steered. Jack set the pace in the bow. He sat up in the webbing seat and he kept the rifle propped against the bow deck.

Wynn felt like they had paddled this stretch of shore now a hundred times. It felt as if they had spent half their lives paddling this piece. If this were really a bad dream, or Hell, they would paddle it for another hundred years. It was not a bad place to have to relive again and again, what with the birches just beginning to yellow, and the brightening day flushing the lake with blue, the tall grasses and the fireweed in so many shades of pink. A place to revisit, to sustain one like Cézanne's mountain. Not.

Jack thought that if he never saw this shoreline for the rest of his life, or one like it, he'd be fine. It was some vortex that kept sucking them back, or the voices were, hers and his. If they'd never heard the voices in that strange fog, they'd be long gone. He wished they were. They needed to get off this damn lake once and for all, get downriver, get to the village and a phone, get the hell out of this country that was starting to feel like very bad luck.

Jack believed in luck. The turning of a card that sent a life in one direction or another. The slip of a single hoof on stone, the sound of two voices in the mist. He believed in it as much as he believed in any other thing, like loyalty or hard work. And sometimes the places that happenstance sent you weren't as vague as a direction, sometimes they were as steel-cast and unforgiving as a set of rails. And sometimes the only way to jump the rails and set a new course was to have a wreck. Right now they needed speed. And he felt some comfort in the rifle propped at his feet; they might need that, too.

~

They quartered into the light wind and made good time. They paddled into the mouth of the outlet and felt the acceleration of the current. They entered the broad right-turning bend and hugged the right shore. Then they came around a ledge of bedrock and they saw the flat horizon line of the falls and beyond it the tops of the trees below, and there was the take-out beach and the tributary and the gap in the willows that was the path of their portage and there was nothing for it but to paddle in. Jack turned on the seat, said, "You got this?"

The current was not too fast and Wynn said, "Sure," and Jack put his paddle behind him and picked up the gun.

~

No sign of a boat. Not on the beach nor in the shade of the trail. They paddled in and hauled out on the shore and Jack said to the woman that they would just be a minute, they were going to take a look, she'd be fine, and she blinked. It was like a semaphore: OK. Jack picked up the rifle and they trotted down the trail.

They could see in the mud that he'd dragged his boat. Maybe he'd hauled it to their campsite on the bluff in front of the cabin. His canoe was polyethylene, the heavy plasticlike material of the synthetic Old Towns; dragging it in the mud and over smooth rocks wouldn't hurt it at all.

They hustled down the now trodden path and burst into the clearing. And stopped dead. It took a second to register: where the pile of gear had been at the edge of the cliff was a scattering of debris, freeze-dried foil packs torn and littered over the grass, two of the blue plastic barrels clawed open and spilled, the other two barrels . . . gone. The ones with their clothes and cooking gear, tarps, pans, warm dry pants and jackets, wetsuits—vanished.

Jack swore. Wynn said, "Bear. Jesus."

Jack didn't say another word. He walked to the exploded food barrels, kicked a lid over with the toe of his boot. It was scratched and mangled. He squatted, tipped up the barrel: empty. Same with the other. Macaroni was scattered in the weeds, the Ziploc torn. The gear had been six feet from the edge of the rock ledge overlooking the falls. Too close maybe. Whatever it was had evidently kicked the two nonfood barrels over the edge. One of the lids lay in the sun. It was scored and gouged.

Neither of them said a word. The implications were dawning: that they had ten days at least of river to go and no food save the two days' worth in their emergency box; that they had an extra person, injured, and no extra warm clothes. Even the wetsuits and the spray skirt that kept water out of the boat were gone. Wynn whistled, a long, downward-sliding exhalation. After a minute he said, "Guess we shouldn't leave food alone in bear country."

Jack straightened and let his eyes wander over the clearing. Then he walked it, zigzagging among the wreckage.

Wynn said, "What are you thinking, Cap?"

"Gimme a minute."

Wynn did. He watched Jack turning the scene over in his mind. Finally Jack said, "I didn't see any bear tracks."

Wynn said, "It's dry out here in the sun. Just rock and scrub."

"Yeah, but even when there's not a bedded print you'll see scrapings where they're getting purchase. I don't know." Jack picked up a lid. "You ever seen a cooler torn open by a bear?"

"No."

"I have."

Wynn walked over. He felt like he was sleepwalking. None of this made sense. "Look," Jack said and knelt, and Wynn knelt beside him. "When a bear tears open a container, to him it isn't no different than a tree. He's been tearing open trees for a million years. A plastic cooler, some poor sonofabitch's car with peanut butter in the trunk—it's all the same to him. His claws dig in somewhere and rip up or down, the way he claws up a root or down on a termite nest or a honeycomb. The claw marks make a continuous line. Look." Jack had the two black plastic barrel lids in his hand. He fitted one, then the other on the mangled top of the barrel and turned them slowly until the one snugged down tight. "The claw marks, if that's what they are, don't line up."

"You think it's something else?"

"Or someone."

"Whoa." Wynn sucked in his breath. It had taken him a while, longer than usual, to follow Jack's train of thought. He said,

"You think Pierre tried to kill his wife. Like you said. And then threw all our shit in the river because we got on the radio and told him we found her alive."

Jack shrugged.

"That's crazy, Cap. Jesus. Out here that'd be like attempted murder. I mean tossing someone's provisions."

Jack turned. Wynn had never seen him look so agitated. Not when he'd decked the man in the bar; not when one of their English profs had said that western ranchers acted tough and independent but were actually on the teat of all sorts of government subsidies.

"It's a death sentence," Jack said. "Or meant to be."

Wynn didn't say anything. He fingered through a few of the empty food packages and said, "I think he's scared of *us*. He seemed panicked. The way he kept his hand on the gun. He thought *we* kidnapped and killed his wife in the fog. Like some *Deliverance* shit. He's not sure, anyway. Or maybe when we didn't come back last night he panicked and took off for help, like he wanted us all to do." Wynn shuddered. "This was a bear. When I imagine a camp torn apart by a bear, it looks just like this." He stood, huffed. "Cap, how many trip accounts did we read where a bear came into camp? It makes sense. Pierre had already made the portage and packed up all his stuff in his boat below and he was waiting for us. Then when the bear tore through camp, he just jumped in his canoe to escape. Figuring we'll follow right after." He rubbed his eyes. "I keep thinking the Texans or whatever they are could have hurt her. I dunno."

"Well, okay," Jack said. One of the things he loved about his buddy was that he cut everyone yards of slack. "All we've got to do is ask *her*. What the fuck happened. But if Pierre did this to her and us, we better be frigging glad he's got a shotgun and we've got a rifle."

Wynn thought about that. If the man did want them dead, with a shotgun and buckshot he'd have to get within fifty or sixty yards. To be sure. With a scoped rifle, if he was good, he could pick them off from a quarter mile.

～

They trotted back up to the beach and the canoe. They couldn't ask her, because her eyes were closed again and her pulse was thready and she'd drifted back into shock.

CHAPTER NINE

They made a fire by the canoe, right on the cobbles of the portage beach. And they wrapped her in the sleeping bags again and heated rocks and warmed her up. They elevated her legs and when she stirred they got her to sip some warm sweet water. It was touch and go; that's what Wynn thought. If she survived the next few days it would be . . . what? A miracle? No, but the odds didn't seem good. If she was going to survive, the next few days would be critical. They needed to keep her in fluids and calories, and more than anything she needed rest. That was the quandary.

They could bust open the door of the little cabin in the clearing and stay for a few days, let her build up her strength. They could forage berries and fish. But. If the fire caught them here they would be toast. Or anywhere up here. From the topo maps the river looked to be pretty narrow for the next forty or fifty miles. Flash-baked. What they didn't want to become. And every day they screwed around here near the lakes was another day closer to harder frosts and snow. She needed rest and they needed to get down the river to the village at the mouth of the bay.

Jack said, "We should get some miles in today."

"I was thinking that. But—"

"If I'm right, Number One Dickhead will be waiting at the next portage. He can't afford to let us pass him."

"Well—"

"It's flat water till Godawful Falls. Twenty-eight miles. She can rest in the boat. The rapid is a short portage like this and an easy beach landing. What the notes say. If he did this, he'll be there."

Wynn said, "Maybe we should pick some blueberries before we take off."

"I was thinking that, too. She's warm in the bags now, we can let her sleep."

"I don't think that's sleep."

"Yeah."

They pulled out the single stainless pot and walked back to the clearing. The cloud shadows moved over it, and over the silvered peeling logs of the cabin walls, and the steel roof, and over the shrubs, the dark swaths of blueberries that roughened the meadow behind.

The swift shadows striped them with running stains that flowed over without a snag and suddenly cooled the air, and were chased upstream by the next sweep of sunlight. Wynn stopped and watched the cloud shadows run and thought that there was something beautiful in the cabin in the clearing in the running sunshine. The crashing of the river had become white noise, and strangely, looking around him, he thought the place was held in a rare silence.

He almost wished they could stay there. Wished that the cabin was stocked with cans of pork and beans, barrels of flour, sugar, rice, salt, packets of dried meat. That there was a saw, two saws, axes, that they could all stay here and rest and put up firewood and hunt a moose and soak the meat in salt brine and hang it to dry on racks. That the three of them could stay there all winter, and she could rest and heal, and they could let Pierre or whoever he was enact whatever drama, whether grief or cover-up. Wynn walked to the edge of the little bluff and looked at the mayhem of the falls.

Ten days out to the village. Eight maybe, if they paddled like demons, but then she would slow them down—on the portages around the big rapids, in the speed with which they could break and make camps and extend their days, and in her need for rest. So maybe more than ten. Jack must have been thinking the same thing, and about the meager amount of food in the box, because he came up beside him and said, "Maybe we should collect more than a potful."

Wynn said, "Good idea."

"I've been thinking about the next portage. Thing is, the book says it's just after a small rock island with a couple of little trees. Says it's an easy take-out, but it doesn't say what the bank's like."

The book was just a printout of a couple of trip blogs, stapled and sealed in a map case. Each of them had one, for redundancy. The most helpful by far was the blog written up by two canoe guides from Pickle Lake who had paddled the river two summers ago. They had a simple sense of humor; they said things like, "Take out just after the bull moose on the left." It made Jack crazy, he thought they were idiots, but Wynn envied people who could wring pleasure from the simplest things. But altogether the trip accounts and the topo map gave them a fairly detailed sketch of what they were in for: a hundred and fifty-two miles altogether, of a big river that flowed north and grew in power as it gathered tributaries big and small. Two more mandatory portages around big falls: about twenty-eight miles to the next one, Godawful Falls. Then eighty-one miles of fast water after that, to the next huge drop and portage at Last Chance Falls, with a couple of bigger rapids between, dangerous but runnable. A large meander in this stretch, northwest to northeast, before the river bent again north and made directly for Hudson Bay as if eager to get home. After Last Chance it was just forty-three miles of swift but mostly flat water to the village and the take-out.

"Thing is," Jack said, "at Godawful we don't know if there's cover. Rocks, trees, maybe a bedrock ledge where Fucker Number One can just go prone and blast us from above. We don't know shit."

"He just panicked. Maybe we'll catch up to him this afternoon. We can talk to him."

Jack didn't answer.

They looked at the rapid. Half the river on the near side poured into a wide chute that unleashed over the first high ledge and battered itself to white on the way down and pummeled the foaming water beneath it in an exploding hole that rolled back on itself. In the surging trough reared a large black log. It buoyed up and was pulled down and buried in froth and bobbed up and flailed for air and was beaten back, held against the falls by the upstream folding of the hydraulic. It made Jack queasy. He looked away. He had long ago trained himself not to think of horses or anything else, but sometimes he did.

"So we'll ask her about what happened when she wakes up," Jack said. "Let's pick a mess of berries now and get going."

~

On their trip so far berry-picking had been the best respite. Maybe the most fun thing they did. Because, unlike with fishing, they had zero ego involved, zero ambition. They hadn't grown up thinking, *I'm going to be the best berry-picker ever,* whereas with fishing and even canoeing they thought that. Berry-picking was like throwing a Frisbee around, or taking a walk up the orchard road, or jumping into the lake and then lying on the sun-warmed stones. It was an achievement-free zone, which Wynn was coming to realize is where most of his joy happened. Making constructions on the riverbank was the same.

Berry-picking was like being a little kid again, crouching in the sun and rolling the berries from fingertips to palm and eating most of them before they reached the cup. They'd done it often on the way across the lakes and Wynn had lost himself every time, daydreamed like a bee-droned bear. They'd met one on Cedar Lake. Wynn had been picking black raspberries, mostly eating them, squatting at the edge of the thicket with the water behind him, and he'd stood at the same time as a black bear on the other side of it. They both swayed, twelve feet apart, about the same height, eye to eye, the bear lifting and moving her nose around, trying to identify the strange and dangerous scent. Odds were she'd probably never met a human before. Wynn had never met a bear that close. They were both surprised. He knew she was a she because a second later two heads popped up out of the bramble, little bear heads, and they looked at him with the curiosity of raccoons. They weren't raccoons, they were this season's cubs, and Wynn's heart jumped because he suddenly knew how much danger he was in. Whatever the smell was, and the maybe strange sight of him, she didn't like it. She snorted and dropped to all fours out of view. He reached for his bear spray and he didn't have it because his pants and belt were lying over the rail of the canoe to dry, he was wearing his long johns, fuck, his hand swiped at air and he knew she had dropped for a charge and would come bursting through the thorns and knock him over. He had only time to bark a shout, to alert Jack, wherever he was, and to pray his buddy had time to break up the fight. He barked and braced and stumbled back and . . . nothing.

Air and sunshine. He saw the tall willows back of the raspberries shake and he knew the bears were hustling away and gone. Maybe it had been the shout. He knew he'd been lucky, and after that he always carried the pepper spray.

And so it was maybe why he'd had no reason to doubt the man's story of losing his wife—he knew how easy it would've been to meet a bear even close to camp. To surprise a bear and be mauled and dragged. Especially in fog. Or even to climb a tree to get away from a bear and slip and fall. He'd read that bears sometimes buried a carcass for later, the way a croc can stuff a kill under a riverbottom log. When he saw the woman's head wound and the bits of earth, his mind had gone from the surprise attack to being half buried by the bear. Did black bears do that? He'd heard of it only with grizzlies. And then, though the man said he'd searched, if he was in shock and scared and blinded by grief he might not have searched that well and have easily missed her. The woods could be very thick. He had been in shock. Why had he been looking straight ahead at the horizon line of the falls and nearly missed the portage? He'd been transfixed. By the danger, maybe. He was traumatized. What if they hadn't yelled and woken him up? *He* might be another casualty, but this one terminal. And so . . . but.

It galloped through Wynn's mind as they circled the cabin and picked. They knelt and filled up the pot and their tied shirts; they gathered with a will and a speed like migrant pieceworkers, the berry-picking that wasn't fun anymore. She had not said more than one word yet, so they didn't know. Jack didn't know either but he was forming a theory. He was gathering evidence and he would indict and convict the man before they even met him again. Wynn wouldn't. It was plausible. It was. A whole handful of possibilities: The Texans with their quiet motor could have stalked the couple in the fog. The poor man Pierre, in the grip of terror, had lost his wife and fled this new bear here by the falls, or fled *them*. Thinking that they had been the ones who had taken her in the mist and were now probably after him.

Wynn picked. There were so many fat berries and now that they weren't eating them he was surprised at the speed and the growing volume. He could grab handfuls. He widened his fingers and raked through the twiggy bunches, the tiny leaves, clawed away the fruit. They were fat and almost blue where the skins were powdery and almost shiny black where the dust had been smudged and rubbed off. His mind raced. He thought about standing up and telling Jack that they needed to slow down, to get reasonable, everything now was going too fast. But what would it accomplish? Their next actions would be the same anyway: they had to get downriver as fast as possible. So. He picked.

~

In an hour they filled their caps, the shirts. Then they filled the single pot with more blueberries, and their two travel mugs. Good. Jack was no fool. He had no illusions that things would just work out, that somehow they would make it out in eight or ten days and would not get weak from hunger and vulnerable to exposure. They needed as many calories as they could get and they could not afford to pass them up. Jack had read the accounts. Of the expeditions that failed, that starved to death, that cannibalized, that lost their lives to cold and hunger. Of the kid who went into the wild and could not gather enough food and lost himself to encroaching lethargy and maybe poisonous berries. More numerous to count—the tragedies. And he had read of the ones that succeeded, sometimes miraculously: of Shackleton, who against all odds did not lose a single man; of Hugh Glass, the mountain man who was mauled badly by a bear and crawled himself through a Rocky Mountain winter to safety. They were not a thousand miles from anywhere, they were something like a hundred and fifty miles upriver from rescue, but they had whitewater to deal with and the onset of early cold, and they did not have all their warm clothes or food, and they had an injured person. Two sleeping bags, one small tent. Well. No more than two could sleep at the same time anyway, because they also might have another threat, and that meant that either he or Wynn would have to sit up at night with the rifle.

Jack thought about that. Lord knows he had been wrong before. Too many frigging times to count. This could have been a bear. But what if it wasn't? What if his warning bells were right and the man was a killer? The only way to stay safe was to assume the worst. Which meant they would have to post a sentry in camp, and they could not both sit up. They would have to take watches. And the one on watch would be sitting by a fire for warmth and the extent of his vision would run to the edge of the firelight. He'd be sitting by a fire, illuminated, and he would not be able to see into the darkness beyond, what? Fifty feet? Sixty? Which meant . . .

His mind turned away from the conclusion and he forced it back. Which meant that most of the time whoever was on watch sitting by the fire was a sitting duck. Could be blasted from the cover of darkness. Especially as the fire burned down, as the watchman got sleepy. And the tent. He felt the goosebumps on his arms. The tent could be snuck up on from the far side, the dark side away from the fire, and the sleepers blown away at close range in their sleep. Then he could sprint forward and blast the surprised watchman as he struggled to swing the rifle and find the target through a scope at night. Which, in a hurry, at close range, is almost impossible.

Fuck. Fuckfuckfuck. The man had them. He had them dead to rights.

They could not travel this way. Waiting to be killed by a spous-icidal maniac. What was the word for a wife-killer? He had to look it up. When . . . when they got back. He did not allow himself to think If.

Plus Wynn was still sleepwalking. He needed to wake up and smell the coffee or they might be toast.

They needed a better plan. Instinctively he knew they could not play defense, not the way they had the night before on the lake. They needed to go on the attack.

~

Jack looked at the sun. It was almost noon. Lots of daylight. The sun didn't set until almost nine p.m. Good. They'd push it. There was no major whitewater until Godawful Falls. If he was waiting for an ambush, it would be there. The map said twenty-eight miles. On a normal trip, taking their time, stopping for lunch, paddling about fifteen miles a day, they'd get there tomorrow afternoon. But this was not a normal trip. Jack thought about the current sliding around the bend here before the falls. It would be about the same below if the river maintained a similar gradi-ent. At this water level—and it was a low year, with the drought, and so the current would be slower—at this flow he figured the river was moving in the flats at about two miles per hour. It would pick up where things got constricted and steeper. He knew that the two of them could paddle 4.5 mph with a loaded boat, no wind. They'd lost gear and food but they had her.

But the canoe would slow down if they had to fight an upstream wind, which typically happened in the afternoons. So say they paddled an average of 3 mph. Add the current: 5 mph total speed, they could get to the portage in six hours. If they loaded up and got moving now, they'd get there before dusk. The sooner they engaged the man, the better, as far as he was concerned. They just had to figure out how.

Offense. A tactical surprise. Something that Number One Shithead would not expect. That's what they had to do. And they had to figure it out in the next six hours.

~

They left her in the spotty sun for last, eyes closed, lying before the fire and whimpering. That was a new development, and it scared Wynn. Could she be unconscious and whimper? He didn't know. Was it her shoulder, or her head, or something inside her? He didn't know and it frightened him.

Jack jerked the canoe to his shoulders and trotted to the clearing and down the steep trail on the other side of it. The path skirted the ledge rock and dropped fast over uneven steps of granite and root to a gravel beach below the falls. Wynn carried the dry bag on his back, the fishing rods, the Pelican box, the rifle. They went back for her and the shirt sacks filled with blueberries. A stretcher would have been the best. They didn't have one and they didn't have time to make one. The portage was too far to carry her in his arms, so Wynn squatted and lifted her into a fireman's carry over his shoulder. He prayed she had no injuries in the soft tissue of her belly. She moaned and he walked as swiftly and smoothly as he could.

CHAPTER TEN

This is what they had gathered on the stones beside the canoe, which Jack slid half into the water:

    1 NRS roll-top dry bag, lg., with shoulder straps

Inside the bag were:

    2 Sierra Designs aqualoft down sleeping bags rated to
        20 degrees F
    2 Therm-A-Rest standard backpacker sleeping pads
    1 Sierra Designs 2-person tent
    1 box 20 ct. Winchester .308 180-grain cartridges,
        minus 6 in the rifle
    2 fleece sweaters, midweight
    2 Gore-Tex rain jackets
    2 shoulder-slung fly-fishing gear bags with fly boxes,
        gink, tippet, etc.

Beside the bag were:

2 fly rods, 9 ft., 5 wt., one Sage (Jack), one Winston (Wynn)
1 Savage 99 .308 lever-action rifle with Leupold 4-12X
    scope
1 Pelican survival and day box

Inside the box were:

    2 emergency blankets
    1 signal mirror
    1 lighter
    1 waterproof match case
    1 magnifying glass
    1 tube fire paste
    6 freeze-dried single-serving meals, assorted—could
        be eaten with cold water if necessary
    1 Ziploc of rolled oats
    1 bottle bouillon cubes
    1 box Lipton teabags
    1 lb. brown sugar
    6 Mars bars
    6 Clif bars
    First aid kit, sm. (gauze, iodine, SecondSkin, mor-
        phine from Wynn's uncle)
    1 stainless steel pot with lid, 3 qt.
    2 stainless travel mugs stamped with the Dartmouth
        Pine and the school logo, *Vox Clamantis in*
        Deserto

Also on the rocks were:

    2 bent-shaft paddles
    3 zip-up life vests
    1 filtered squeeze water bottle, 1 qt.

On their persons they each carried:

> 1 can bear spray in Cordura belt clip
> 1 Leatherman
> 1 clip knife

And they had maybe twenty pounds of blueberries. They emptied their caps and the pot into the improvised shirt sacks.

That was it. Step back and one sees on the rocks of the beach one blue duffel-size bag, one plastic box the size of a large camera box, two fishing rods, and a rifle. And a couple of bulging tied undershirts full of berries, like two lumpy pillows. Not much.

They wouldn't have had any of it if Jack hadn't been thinking fast.

This is how they loaded the Wenonah nineteen-foot Itasca expedition canoe:

They propped the dry bag just aft of the center thwart. They lashed it in as best they could with its two shoulder straps.

They lowered the woman into the boat and let her lean against the bag as a backrest, and she sat on Jack's life vest. She was facing aft. They were a bit stern-heavy, but it would have to do. They decided they wanted her facing backward so someone could see her face and watch her. Also, after what she'd been through they thought it might be better, if she woke up, to see someone she could easily talk to rather than watch the bowman's back. They unslung her left arm for a minute and worked her into her own life vest and zipped it up. It was just flat swift water for the next twenty-eight miles, but if for some unforeseen reason they flipped, neither had confidence that she could swim.

The Pelican box, thankfully, still had its own short cam strap looped to the handle so they strapped it to the thwart right behind the bow paddler. They leaned the fly rods beside her on the starboard side, rod tips angled up and forward. They would not get in the way of the bow paddler, who they decided would be Jack from now on. He was the shooter and if they needed to shoot from the boat Wynn could navigate and steer from the stern. And then the rifle went up in the bow, leaning against the bow deck, leather strap clipped to the bow carry handle with a carabiner. Jack thought about it and went back to the dry bag and unclipped and unrolled it against her back and fished out the ammo box and picked six more cartridges out of the plastic holder and slipped them into the front pocket of his Carhartt pants.

They laid the tied shirts filled with blueberries in the completely open section of boat between center and forward thwarts, where they looked like sad limbless sacks of contraband. They laid them on Wynn's open life vest to lift them off the hull in an effort to keep them as dry as possible. They'd need the shirts tonight. The breeze was picking up and it smelled strongly of smoke now and the clouds were flying, but they were getting more widely spaced, like fleets of ships scattered by storm. It was clearing. Tonight looked to be cloudless, and if it was, it would probably frost hard again and it would be cold. They'd need every layer they had. Now they were in their light under-shirts, which in the cool breeze was just tolerable, but they knew they'd warm up as they paddled.

They did. They glanced at each other and Wynn slid the boat bow-first farther into the water and held it steady as Jack climbed in; then, in case the woman could hear, he said to her, "We're going to get going now, okay? We have easy flat water all day today, we're just going to move downriver." Her eyelids fluttered and he saw that the swelling there was calming down and that the blood in her right ear had dried. And then he gave a strong shove and hopped in, a practiced jump, and the boat buoyed with what seemed like relief, and they were floating free across the pool. They slid over the eddy line and the steady current turned them downstream in a wide arc and they dug in and began paddling north.

CHAPTER ELEVEN

They got hot. They paddled hard. Almost thirty miles on a flat-water current was a long way even for them. Because the river slowed and expended itself in unexpected wide coves. From which loons called as they passed—the rising wail that cracked the afternoon with irrepressible longing and seemed to darken the sky. The ululant laughter that followed. Mirthless and sad. And from across the slough or from far downstream the cry that answered.

And the eagles. They seemed to mark the canoe's progress from the gray spires of dead spruce, spaced downriver like watchmen on some lost frontier, sometimes just the unmistakable shape of the hooded predator, sometimes a scraggly limb and a huge stick nest.

They made time. They were strong paddlers and they lay into a steady rhythm and they stuck to the center of the river where a blast from a shotgun would be less likely to kill them. They stuck to the center even when the current was stronger and faster on the outside of a bend. It was mostly wide enough, the river here, between the banks. He'd have to be very good or lucky to make the shot. Wynn steered to the middle because Jack motioned every time they got too close to a bank. He didn't have the energy to argue. Wynn still thought the notion crazy; he thought it much more likely that the man needed helpers, not adversaries.

There had been the falls, but the river didn't truly drop off the Canadian Shield—the vast plateau of ancient bedrock that covered much of northern Canada—for another fifty miles or so, and when it did it would pick up speed and maybe narrow before it widened again on its way to the bay. Here they could stay thirty yards from either bank. Maybe enough, maybe not.

They paddled. They leaned into the work. They would get their best sprint on their knees, but they knew they had a long haul and so stayed in the seats for comfort and reached for the long stroke. They each used an alder and basswood paddle made by the master Mitchell in New Hampshire and the blades bent from the shaft to keep the stroke farther forward, where it was strongest. The most efficient stroke was all in front of the paddler, the blade lifting out of the water when it reached the hip.

Jack set a hard pace and they paddled in perfect sync. On the lakes above they'd had all the time in the world and so had paddled expedition-style, with the sternman finishing his stroke with a slight twist of the shaft and the paddle's power face arcing outward, the J-stroke. It kept the canoe straight. It was invented long ago because physics dictated that a stroke in the stern had much more steering power than a stroke in the bow, so if the sternman paddled, say, on the right side, starboard, the boat would always be turning left, to port. And so the little bit of twist and outward pressure at the end of the stern stroke acted like a rudder and checked the tendency to veer away. But the J-stroke took time. And that seemed long ago, that feeling of leisure, of taking their time. Of making the crossings at their own pace. Of drifting half the afternoon along the shadow of some ledge and casting for lake trout. That was before they climbed the hill on the island and saw the glow. Before they heard the couple arguing in the fog. That was another life.

Now they had to make tracks, so they paddled marathon-style. Every eighth stroke or so, Wynn uttered *"Hut!"* and they switched sides. It meant they zigged and zagged slightly as they progressed, but the stroke rate was much higher. They moved much faster. And it took a lot more concentration. Still, Jack kept his eyes scanning ahead as far as he could see, all along the banks on either side. He was a hunter, and he'd trained himself most of his life to pick out movement and anomalous shapes. He didn't have to think about it. He could spot a buck browsing in the shadows on some northern New England river long before Wynn, even with patient directions. ("Whoa, look at that sucker. Must be a six-by-six. See, under the beech." "No." "Two o'clock, see?" "No." "He just stepped, there, in the shadow just to the right of the big silver tree." "Uh—I know what a beech is!" "Are you fucking blind?" "I think I see him." "No you don't. Three o'clock!" . . . Like that.) Jack had the honed sight of a hunter, but Wynn had a lot more whitewater experience and he could see lines through rapids and holes where Jack just saw mayhem, so Wynn figured they were even. Jack looked now for Pierre.

He was getting hot paddling and the muscles of his back and arms had the burn he knew he could sustain all day, and his breath came with the steady chuff of a train, and Jack made himself look. For the man or his green canoe. He let his eyes run up and down the banks, the shores of the wider bays. Why couldn't the boat have been red, or bright yellow? He thought they made the Old Towns in those colors. Nope, it had to be green, the color of the woods, as if the man had been planning on stealth.

The river widened. The occasional eskers that made the long ridged hills got farther and farther apart, the country flatter. That ten miles could make such a difference. Maybe it was a local thing, the topography. What he didn't want was high banks, a constriction, where the man could reach them with a fusillade from good cover, and now the river was obliging by spreading itself into reaches of water that were like small lakes of their own. But still. The walls of mixed woods, of pine, spruce, fir, tamarack, birch, they were bulwarks of brooding silence that could shadow any intention. He thought of Conrad again, one of his favorites, of *Heart of Darkness* and what the masking forest meant to the thrashing steamer in that glorious story. Nothing but danger.

The woman slept. Seemed to. She leaned back against the dry bag, eyes closed, propped in the corner of the bag and the gunwale. She sat on the life vest but her legs stretched out on the hull, where there was always water sloshing, and Wynn noticed that her pant legs were getting wet. They no longer had the big sponge they used to sop up what they called the bilge water—it was always there, water dripped off the paddles as they switched sides and collected—they'd have to cut the limbs of fir trees to make her a dry bed. They'd do it at the next stop.

The next stop. It didn't matter, it was a long way off. Paddling in rhythm like this, at high cadence, Wynn noticed that after a while he barely had to utter *"Hut"* before Jack switched and the paddles swung up and forward in perfect synchrony and their four hands changed position on shaft and handle midair and the blades hit the water at exactly the same moment: he could feel the canoe surge with the next stroke without a hitch. Smooth.

They paddled in perfect concert, and Wynn also noticed that he could hear Jack's breathing on the upstream breeze and that his own had slowed over the first miles and fallen into time with Jack's and that they now breathed in unison. He also noticed that somehow in the concord of effort he forgot himself. The pain of it. What would have hurt and held his thoughts on when it might end, on when they could pull over and rest, or slow down—now because he and Jack moved the slender boat almost as one engine, somehow it freed him. His mind untethered and his attention ranged. He noticed that she was not asleep. She was breathing steadily, he could see the rise and fall of the life vest, but every once in a while she would shudder and gasp and her right hand resting on her thigh would clench. Her eyes would flutter open and, if he was watching, would meet his. Hazel green eyes he could see now. And there was something there: gratitude, maybe. A frustration that she couldn't speak or help. Sadness. But she didn't make another sound. That was the most unnerving. The gasp trailed off in the faintest whimper and that was it. No moan or cry. Not good. Wynn wondered again if something was broken inside and how much.

He also noticed that despite the swelling, which had lessened since yesterday, and despite the bruising on her face and neck, she had fine features. High cheekbones and a straight nose. Her hair in the braid was glossy dark and streaked with russet. He imagined that she might be pretty; she was, for sure. Or not. Something stronger. She was strong. He could feel it in her every action and response, the tenacious will to live, even the desire not to be a burden. He paddled, lost in some fugue of rhythm and effort, and was startled when she convulsed again, and whimpered, and he winced himself and felt the heat flood his neck. When her eyes opened and quieted and settled on him, he said, "Maia? I'm Wynn. We're gonna keep moving. We're all gonna get out of here." And he thought she might just have nodded before her eyes closed again.

~

They had paddled for almost four hours. The smell of smoke seemed to be getting stronger, ranker, with every mile. Not good. The sun was more than halfway to the trees on the west bank. Except for Wynn's promise, no one had spoken. Jack finished five strokes on the left and laid the paddle across the gunwales and they drifted. Wynn let out a breath of relief and set the paddle against the seat. They glided. The boat seemed to take pleasure in it, to expend itself, too, with a long exhalation as the upstream wind turned it in a gentle arc to the west. They were in a wide reach. There was stony bank to their left and a broad cove on the east, densely wooded. Jack turned around in the bow seat. "How is she?" he said under his breath. Wynn shrugged. Jack read it as, *Not so good.*

"Is she waking up?"

"I dunno. A little. She's whimpering."

"We should haul out," Jack said. "We should take a look and get some food in her. In us, too. She might have to pee. I know I do." When they were by themselves they knelt on the seat and peed over the rail. Now they both felt shy about doing it, even though their passenger was unconscious most of the time.

"How many miles do you think we've gone?"

Jack looked at the sun. He ran his eyes over the shore and gauged the progress of the current. With the wind in their faces and drifting, they barely moved. "Eighteen. Twenty."

"Damn."

"I know."

"Eight or ten to go."

Wynn drank from the squeeze bottle, unscrewed the cap, refilled it. He tossed it to Jack. "You think we should pull out here?"

Jack drank. With the bottle tipped up he let his eyes run over the close bank, the left, the ledge rock and forest. He looked across to the right shore, far across the cove to the line of dense woods where half a dozen ducks flew fast over the trees and out across the water. "He won't risk us getting past him, like I said."

Wynn waited.

"I think we're good right here. He wouldn't be at some random spot, right?" Jack said.

"I guess. I don't think we need to be playing army."

Jack had the bottle halfway to his mouth. He lowered it. His eyes were flat.

"You think we're playing?"

"I'm not sure, to tell you the truth."

They drifted. Jack held his eyes on Wynn and Wynn could not tell what he was thinking, except that the *Gimme a minute* was unspoken.

Jack took his minute and said, "Your problem is you've got faith. In everyone, in everything. The whole universe. Everyone is good until proven bad. You're kinda like a puppy."

That stung.

"Thing is, Wynn, this fucker might have just tried to kill his wife." He tossed the half-full bottle back. It hit Wynn in the chest but he caught it. "If he did, now he's gonna try to kill *you*."

Wynn didn't know what to say. The Jack in the bow resembled the Jack he knew, but. If he'd seen him like this, it had never been aimed in his direction. Wynn said, "Well, if he did it, why didn't he just shoot her? Why didn't he just shoot us, for that matter? When he first landed?"

Jack grimaced; he didn't want to be anywhere near the man, much less inside his head. He said, "He didn't shoot her because he's chickenshit. He thought he'd knock her out with a rock and bury her in the moss and duff and let the cold and wet and the animals take care of the rest. Too cowardly to brain his wife. Almost worked, too. Also, if he shot her and anyone ever did happen to find her they'd find a blast hole somewhere and maybe a slug, his slug. He didn't shoot us because we surprised him. He wasn't expecting us. We have a rifle and he's got a shotgun and there's two of us, and anyway he's got to think it through. He doesn't want us to get out of here, any of us. But he'd rather dump our shit and let the river and the weather and hunger take care of us. He's not a born killer. And if he has to deal with us himself, he wants to think it through and pick his spot. Make it clean."

"His spot," Wynn murmured.

"Ambush. He didn't ambush us back there because it was too open and spread out with two of us. He doesn't have the balls for a firefight. He'll let the river finish us, but if he has to, he'll try to take us where we're crammed tight and very close."

Wynn shook his head. "There was an accident. Bad. Then there was a bear. Now there's some dude trying to run the river solo and so traumatized he can't see straight. He needs help as much as we do. Jesus."

"Look, Big, maybe it was a bear. I've been dead wrong before. Maybe the bear shouldered our gear barrels into the river. Maybe she did fall out of a tree. But if she was some accident and this was a bear, where the fuck is Pierre?"

"That's just crazy."

Jack spat into the current. He said, "Our friend here will tell us. She's not saying, but she will. We can cling to the bear theory or the fall-out-of-a-tree theory all we want, but meanwhile he took our food and dumped our shit in the river and he's trying to kill us, too. And the sonofabitch has a gun." Jack touched the rifle in the bow, the gesture almost unconscious. He scanned the far shore. "Lucky fucking thing he doesn't have an ought-six or we'd be dead by now, guarantee it," he murmured. He turned back to Wynn. "Let's say you're right. Pierre is off his meds. Pierre is panicked. Pierre is afraid *we're* the killers and took off. Pierre just needs to be talked down, won over. Oh yeah, and that was *another* bear that scattered all our food and threw our shit in the falls. Bears everywhere—*man*. Good. Good then. Awesome. Everyone really *is* good and fair, go figure. But—" He snagged the tin of Skoal out of his pants pocket and twisted the lid, took a dip. "We really don't wanna find out we're wrong with buckshot to the chest."

"I'm not saying everyone's an angel. It could've been the two drunks."

"I don't think those guys could stalk a pine tree. Anyway, you're the doc—she's waking up, right? Why don't you ask her?"

"Not really."

"Not really like she's not waking up, or not really like you don't want to stress her out by asking if we're going to get shot at any minute?"

Wynn winced. "Why are you making me the bad guy?"

"You're not the bad guy. Definitely not. The bad guy seems to be in a category of his own. I just don't know what category to put someone in who I think is my friend and is trying to get me killed." Jack picked up his paddle. "Let's go to shore and have lunch."

~

After that nobody spoke. They found a low spot in the granite ledge rock and scraped up onto it. The canoe was Kevlar but it had an extra layer like a bow plate for that purpose. They never treated it like an eggshell, or a canvas canoe. It was made to get beat up, which is a little how they saw themselves. Okay to get roughed up, but not by each other. That's what Wynn thought as he ran the painter to an alder and tied it off. They'd always been back-to-back.

When they got to the canoe to lift her out, Jack said, "Hey, I'm sorry. If I'm amped, I just want us all to get down this river safe. All three of us." Jack looked away and Wynn suddenly thought of Jack's mother. The other river, when one of the three hadn't made it out alive. Jack hadn't told him the story until they had known each other for over a year. Jack said, "I just think we've gotta be prepared."

Wynn said, "It's okay. I get it."

They carried her to a bench of grassy duff and laid her down. Her lower pant legs were wet where they'd been awash, and so was her seat. A sharp urine smell lingered. Jack exhaled.

Without a word he began stripping off her pants and Wynn took off his. He always wore light wool long underwear—Jack had teased him that his hair would start growing through it, that they'd have to cut it off by the end of the season. They left her in the sun and Jack walked to the river and rinsed out her pants and underwear and spread the pants over willow branches. He dipped and wrung the underwear like a rag and came back and squatted beside her and whispered, "I'm going to clean you up." And he did. When he was done he took the underwear back to the river and rewashed it and hung it on the branches. Wynn stripped his wool long johns and buckled his canvas pants back on and worked her feet into the woolies and tugged them up over her legs and hips. This had to change, he thought. She needed to wake up enough to drink some water, to eat something. If she didn't, she would slip back into shock and die of exposure.

Jack went to the canoe and heaved up one of the tied shirts. Must be fifteen pounds. He carried it to them. Then he went back for a cup and a spoon and the water bottle.

"We'll make a mash," he said. Wynn nodded. "Do you think you can get her to drink a little?"

"I don't know. I don't know if it's safe to try to wake her."

"Is it safe to let her go days with nothing?"

"No."

The blueberries had warmed inside the shirt, in the sun. The fragrance made their mouths water. Jack poured a handful into the cup and mashed them with the spoon. Added a trickle of water and stirred the slurry. "Wanna see if she will drink something first?" he said.

"Okay." Wynn placed one hand under her head along the band of the wool hat and asked Jack with a look if he could come around the other side and lift her back. They sat her up and she moaned, very faintly. "Got her?" Wynn said. He let go and jogged to the canoe, unstrapped the dry bag and brought it back, propped her up. She took shallow rapid breaths and uttered a soft whine. She seemed to be terrified or in pain. It made Wynn think of Leo back home, his black Lab, when he was having a nightmare. Her eyes fluttered open for a second and closed. Fuck. They really needed her in a hospital right now, probably in ICU, probably getting prepped for surgery. Who knew what was going on. Well, getting some nourishment inside her could not make it much worse. He bent to her ear and said, "Maia. Maia? Can you hear me?" A catch in the whimper, as if some thread of comprehension had snagged. Then a tentative moan like a question. "We've got to get some food and water in you, okay? It's important." Was it important? Without knowing if she had internal injuries, they couldn't know whether feeding her would do more damage. Could it? He wasn't a doctor. He felt his own panic rise up. Wynn had taken a wilderness EMT course one spring in the mountains of western North Carolina. He had learned to stop bleeding and splint a fracture, how to lower someone down a cliff on a backboard. None of it had prepared him for this.

Jack held the water bottle and his demeanor had not changed. He had tugged calves out of bloody wombs with a chain and put down a bellowing cow in the snow with a shot in the forehead when his ministrations had failed. None of it was fun, and it was neither good nor bad.

She took in one long volcanic breath and cried out, a sharp report of pain, and her eyes opened. *"Try,"* she said. Her first clear word since they'd found her. Wynn tipped up the bottle and trickled water into her half-open mouth and she blinked for a pause and he repeated until the bottle was empty. Then Jack spooned her the blueberry mash. She ate half a cup, good. The effort seemed to exhaust her. Before Jack could ask her what he needed to know, she rolled her head back and her eyes shuttered closed.

They ate blueberries themselves until they were bloated. They knew they'd get the shits, but what choice did they have? They drank their fill of water and then Wynn carried her back to the boat and they shoved off.

Replay of the morning. Steady paddle. Except that now their muscles were tired and sore and the wind came in flat gusts upstream or quartered across from the northwest and then they could smell the smoke with the intensity of a campfire that blows in your face. More acrid and dense, though; more char. It smelled like devastation. And then, in late afternoon, they saw the first flocks of birds.

They were haphazard squadrons of songbirds, forest birds, colorless, in chaotic formations, mostly silent and fast winging east across the river. There were chickadees and tiny warblers and waterthrush, olive flycatchers, kinglets and crows. The wrens and warblers cried and peeped as they flew in a chorus of constant questioning, maybe panic, and the reedy squeaks rained down like gusts of weightless hail. Then came waxwings, woodpeckers, flickers flashing yellow. And the larger lake birds, the rare heron the color of fog beating out the slow cadences of lunar time, the cranes, the loons in twos and threes, sailing overhead with the singular swiftness of arrows. No raptors yet, which the boys found curious. They watched with speechless fascination and often found themselves stilled, not paddling, drifting against the wind and gawking at the sky. Also, it could not be good. Neither said a word.

When they paddled they paddled hard, as hard as they had ever done. Jack did not want to get there in the dark with no options but to sit out the freezing night with no fire—he wanted to devise a plan, he wasn't sure what, and have enough light to enact it. The sun lowered to the tops of the tallest spruce and made a molten fringe of the trees; it seared and spindled them as if they had already burned. The temperature dropped. Wynn dug out the sleeping bags and covered her and they kept paddling into the frail light, the river surface gone to slate, then a casting of flat burnished silver that tilted into the uneven darkness of dusk.

They passed the rock island with the two trees and were swept into a tight left bend and they heard the buffeting rush of the rapid carried up the half mile of river like the sound of wind. The river began to straighten and they knew that soon on the right they would see a small shale beach pale in the twilight. Their portage. That's what the book had said. Jack turned suddenly and very sharply said, "Head to the right bank. Pull out. Now."

"What?"

"Do it, Wynn. Crank to the right. Hurry the fuck up."

"That's steep bank." It was. "Nothing but trees." It was. "We've got to get her out, the easier the better, and lay her down. Get her warm. The book said there's an easy beach landing."

"Head in. There."

"*No.* Jesus, what's wrong with you? She's gonna go back into sh—"

The word died in his mouth. Jack had set his paddle against his seat. He had picked up the rifle and he was aiming it at Wynn.

CHAPTER TWELVE

"I'm not bluffing. Brother, you point the bow to the bank, there." Jack tossed his head toward a shallow cove and an eroded cut where maybe a game trail ramped into the water from thick woods. "Point it and get us there. *Now.*"

For a second Wynn was stunned. He thought, *Has he gone fucking crazy?* But he did. He ruddered hard and reached forward and laid into the stroke, a stroke to keep them moving cross-current, and they bumped the bank and Jack hopped out with the painter rope and the rifle slung over his shoulder. He tied it off fast to a young fir and jerked his head toward the woods and the thickening darkness. "Get out. Leave her. Won't be long. Hurry up. I got the boat." The canoe spun stern into the bank and Jack crouched and steadied it as Wynn shimmied forward, around and over her, and hopped out. He was towering over Jack and he might have shoved him into the water but he didn't. Jack could come up shooting, who knew what. What the hell was going on? The day at its end—burnished in the last reluctant light—seemed to warp and twist and twang like a bent saw blade.

Wynn stood over Jack. "What the fuck," he whispered.

Jack glanced up at him. "I know, Big. Just frigging follow me. You'll thank me." The tone had softened. He sounded like his friend. "Let's go."

Wynn did, follow him. What choice did he have? Into the true night under the trees, downriver, and out to the margin of brush along the bank where they found another game trail, probably moose. They moved as fast as they could and could see enough to make out the shapes of river stones in the dirt, the tufts of grass and moss, the orange bark of the bigger spruce, barely ruddy in the dusk. They came to another scrim of trees and the sky opened and lightened beyond them and they knew they had come to the clearing of the take-out, what must be the opening of a beach, a camp, an overlook. They could hear the rapid now as a proximal thunder.

Jack put his finger to his lips and unslung the rifle and they moved forward slowly. Crouched in twilight like two predators, they pushed through a stand of tall grass and looked down on a sandy bench with two old fire rings. The bench was fifteen feet above the water and beyond it they could see the whitewater of the heavy rapid fluorescing like snow. A trail wound from the camp around the cut-rock overlook down to a small gravel beach they could partly see. The beach was the mandatory take-out for the portage around the falls. And at the edge of the rock ledge, looking directly down on the gravel bar, lay a man. A man in a broad-brimmed safari hat.

"What the fuck is he doing?" Wynn whispered right against Jack's ear.

"He's holding his 12-gauge shotgun is what he's doing. Waiting for us. You can see it in his hands. His hands are fucking shaking—you can see it from here."

Wynn huffed. It was an exhalation of surprise, of shock, of profound disappointment, as if he'd just looked down at his compass and the needle was spinning. Pierre was not spinning or moving, he was preternaturally still. "Where's all his shit?" Wynn whispered. "His camp?"

"It's all packed in the canoe below. Ambush, flee. That's his plan. It's not a very good one. A search party will surely come. I guess he might be thinking to hack us all up into bits with his ax and throw everything in the river. Send the canoe over the falls so whatever gear is left looks like a flip. The headline will be 'River Accident.'"

Wynn had no response. He'd had the wind knocked out of him playing hockey and it usually took a few panicked seconds to find his breath. He felt like that now.

Jack was on one knee. He brought up the scoped rifle and twisted his left arm through the leather sling and sighted.

"What do you wanna do?" Wynn said, more loudly. "Shoot him where he lies?"

Jack had his eye to the scope and the sling twisted tight against his arm. "What do *you* wanna do?" he said. "Truss him up and carry him for a week down the river, back to back with the wife he tried to kill?"

Jack felt Wynn's hand grip his right arm. Jack's right forefinger lay over the trigger guard. Wynn shook him. "Whoa!" Wynn whispered, urgent. "We've gotta talk to him. We've gotta know. He still might think we killed her, he still might be scared of *us*. Or those Texans." He didn't know. "*Jack!* Fuck." Wynn shook him. "You can't just murder him! We've gotta confront him."

Jack lifted his eye off the scope and studied his buddy. The dusk was thickening. If they were going to shoot anybody through a 4-12X scope, it would have to be soon. Okay, Wynn needed closure, clarity, whatever the hell, let's go. "Okay, Wynn. Fuck it. This is on you. This is it. On three we'll move down the slope slow. I'll cover him. We'll get as close as we can so he knows he's cooked."

Wynn nodded.

"One, two, three." They stood. They pushed out of the trees and the tall grass and stepped down the slope. Jack carried the rifle in front of him. It was grass, moss, rocks. Pierre was sixty feet away. Wynn stepped on a sloping root and his right foot skidded along it and he loosed a rock and nearly stumbled. The rock clacked on the stones below. And Pierre jumped. He wheeled, crouched, and Jack saw the muzzle of the shotgun flash. Spit flame. And the explosion at close quarters. Branches and leaves tore behind them to their left. Jack shouldered the rifle and sighted. He had him; Pierre lunged for the trail. Jack swung and led him and fired. He might have, might have nailed him. But Pierre had leapt behind the outcrop. It was a perfect shot. Jack was running. Running down the slope and looking for the kill as he would an elk. The trail vanished behind the guard rock of exposed ledge. He ran. He would find the man crumpled behind it. He would have zero remorse. He half turned once to see if Wynn was hit. Wynn was behind him, good. Jack loosed his feet down the slope and jumped to the sand on the bench and brought the rifle up again, both eyes open, and came around the ledge and—

Nothing. If the man had been hit it hadn't been fatal. Jack blinked. Fuck. The man's hat lay on the sand of the trail like a giant fungus. Jack ran. He fast-stepped down the rocky steps and sand of the narrow trail. It dropped to the river and he leapt onto the broken shale of a beach and there was the canoe. The canoe on the black current, the man a shadow now, the boat sliding past a point of granite into the tight right bend. Jack lifted the rifle, both eyes open, and half sighted through the dim scope, the shadow sliding across it, and he fired, the blast of flame, and the canoe and the man slid past the rock and out of sight. Into the charry night.

~

Because that's what it reeked of. Charcoal. They could not see the fire, no plumes clouded the stars, no glow like some city crowned the trees, but it reeked of burned-out forest and scorched ground, and all night they heard the flurry and peeps of birds flying over.

CHAPTER THIRTEEN

Jack did not speak. Whatever jeopardy they had been in before, they were in more now. Pierre would know with certainty where they would camp—here—and he could ambush them while they slept or sat by the fire. But they needed a fire. She was shivering again. She needed hot liquid, they would make up one of the freeze-dried meals and feed it to her; she needed sustenance and rest. So. Jack would let Wynn care for her and he would set a perimeter and patrol it.

The night was clear. No clouds tonight, no moon, but a swarm of stars like sparks, against which flew the high wind-strewn shadows of the birds. Steady wind from the north. The stars illuminated the night enough. Good. If the man had gone only just around the bend and was working his way back for an attack, he could only come along the ledge rock or out of the line of trees to the east. The trees were back far enough that he would not be able to shoot from cover. Good.

They built a fire because they had to. They wrapped her in the bags again and warmed stones and when she came halfway to consciousness they fed her spoonfuls of sweetened and warmed water and the hot meal they'd made in its foil pack. Then they laid her back down and she slept. They ate blueberries and felt the exhaustion rise in their bodies like a ground fog and they knew they needed to catch fish or some other animal. Wynn had hunted in Vermont, but Jack didn't trust him to secure the camp from a human attacker: Wynn might see the man crawl out of the woods and maybe even put him in the crosshairs, but he wasn't sure he would shoot him. Wynn would want to ask him why he was so scared; maybe they could work everything out, none of this could be as base and horrific as it seemed. So Jack watched Wynn set up the tent and told him to take the first sleep, he'd sit with her by the fire, but he did not intend to wake him. He braced himself to keep vigil all night.

She slept. They'd tugged the wool hat down over her ears and pillowed her head with a pile of fir needles and covered those with the hoods of the sleeping bags. Less blocky and hard than one of the life vests. They had talked about whether to put her on her side so she wouldn't aspirate, but they hadn't seen her have any trouble breathing yet, or vomit or spit up in her sleep or coma or wherever she drifted, and so they thought she would be more comfortable on her back. They would watch her, though. Jack sat on a rock covered with his own life vest for warmth because the night was cold. He laid a couple of larger sticks on the fire and looked at her face. The swelling had come down today and he could see the planes of her cheeks for the first time, the bruising now a blush of pink edged with purple or black like something slowly smoldering. Maybe he thought that way because he could smell the burn, strong when the wind shifted a little more from the west. It was somehow consoling, not creepy, with the birds flying over. They were just reedy scatterings of sound over the rush of the rapid, and shadows more of movement than substance against the stars; they were saving themselves from whatever cauldron and it made him feel that they, the three of them, were not alone. One of his classmates at high school in Granby had become a hotshot firefighter in Idaho and had died in the infamous White River Complex when seven firefighters had been pinned against a ridge in a sudden wind shift and overrun. The boy had deployed his personal fire shelter against the ground and Jack thought he must have prayed as he huddled inside it, blind, and heard the trees exploding. He was nineteen.

He and Shane had lost cattle twice in fires. He never again wanted to be on horseback and in the path of a burn while he and his father tried to haze cow-calf pairs off the mountain. All they had to worry about now was themselves. Themselves. His mind was wandering and he forced himself to scan the edge of the trees back of the clearing, which he could see well enough by starlight. And the head of the trail, which was only thirty feet away.

He scanned, but still he wondered what had really happened. Had the man really swung a rock at his wife's skull in some rage, or in some more calculated blindside, and then chickened out from strangling or braining her and just covered her with moss and duff where she lay? They must have planned the trip together—they had been out for some days already, out on the lakes because he and Wynn had not heard any planes. So the couple were functional partners at least in the sense of the barest logistics, in moving the canoe over water, in making camp. They had planned the trip together, packed together, must have shared the route-finding, they were in God's country, among moose and loons, had slept under benign constellations—what could have brought them to blows, to murder? No telling, truly. Nothing but woods, then taiga, then tundra and mudflats, then the sea, nothing but the cries of birds, maybe coyotes, maybe wolves, sweeps of rain, the mutterings of wind for hundreds, even thousands of miles in any direction. Whatever malevolence the couple had ignited they had brought with them. That puzzled him. Why come so far if you were doing so badly? As people, as husband and wife? Why come way the hell up here?

Fuck: was that something moving against the wall of trees? No? No. He needed to stay on top of it, he was getting drowsy. Exhausted muscles and not much food weren't helping. He thought of the pale hungry Windigo that stalked this country: it flickered at the corner of the eye but could never be truly seen; no matter how many people it consumed, it was never satiated, it stayed gaunt and voracious. He reached for the sack of blueberries and ate another handful. How long could you live on these? How long could you shit your guts out every day? They needed some meat.

He stood, stretched his arms, slung the rifle, and stepped off fifteen feet to pee. He was facing the river and he could smell the crashing water, the sediment in it and the spray, and he could see what the sluice of turbulence was doing to the dark. It was shredding the night and maybe his peace of mind. At least the violence was keeping him awake.

His mind drifted to the other violent and beautiful river. He had forced himself to ride his quarterhorse Duke back up the canyon of the Encampment just once. It was the summer before college, seven years after his mother had died there, and he had taken his father's truck and the little two-horse trailer that hitched to the ball, not the gooseneck, and he had loaded Duke and they had driven north through Steamboat to Walden and turned up the North Platte and then forked up into the Encampment, and he had taken the Highline Road through the steep hills of lodgepole and spruce woods to Horseshoe Park and the top of the canyon. He didn't take a packhorse and he didn't tell his father where he was going and Shane didn't ask. He and Duke camped in the park as the family had seven years before, and he put the gelding out on a picket—he wasn't worried about him getting tangled up in the line, he was a mellow camper—and Jack fell asleep in his bag in the back of the truck with the sound of Duke chomping wheatgrass and his occasional snort and a couple of crickets. The low slip of the river. He made himself think about nothing. In the morning he made a fire and made coffee and ate a power bar and then he saddled up and they rode. It was mid-August and the little river was low and green over the myriad colors of the stones. It flowed gently in the flats and in the riffles it fell with the capricious release of a man whistling as he rode. So different from the June highwater throb and surgings of that other time. He rode through the sage and grass clearings along the bank, the paintbrush and lupines, and into the big trees, and when they got to the true gorge and the river spilled away from the trail and they were high above it, he pushed Duke, carefully, but did not pause, and when he got to the sloping rock slab he was sure was the one and looked down into the gorge at the ledgy drop that was all boulders now—nothing like the white torrent—he clucked twice and urged his horse across and they rode out of the canyon. That was it. He did not make himself ride back up. He talked to a lady in Encampment who had two horses in her yard and she let him turn Duke in, and he hitched a ride with two fishermen back up to his truck. He took one more look at the river running low and clear and drove down to town to pick up his horse. He had hay and oats in the trailer and he fed and watered Duke and loaded him up and drove home. He cried on the way. Once or twice, maybe more. At Hot Sulphur Springs he cried so hard the road blurred. He didn't know why, why then. He never told his father.

Now he blew out a long breath and shivered and zipped himself up. He stretched and looked up at the sky. Across the river and downstream, high up, somewhere over where the fire should be, there was a pale cloud that drifted and elongated and accordioned into a high curtain of softest light, and as he watched, it spread silently across the northern sky. It pulsed with inner radiance as if alive and then poured itself like a cascade to the horizon and shimmered with green. A pale green cataract of something scintillant that spread across an entire quadrant and sang as it fell with total absence: of sound, of substance, of water or air. In the week before, they had sometimes seen what looked like the faintest moving clouds, but not this. Now an arc of greener light shot from the top of the falls and jumped the current of the Milky Way and ignited a swirl of pink in the southeast that humped and crested like a wave. Jack shivered. The northern lights had just enacted what the heat and sparks would do when they jumped the river. It was like a portent—more: a preview—and it was as if every cantlet and breath of the night was filled with song—and silent. It was terrifying and unutterably beautiful.

Wynn had told him that the Cree and other northern peoples thought of the lights as the spirits of the dead who looked down in judgment of the living and so when the aurora appeared the people kept their bad children inside so as not to offend the ancestors. Jack thought that was funny. He figured a bad child, or adult for that matter, was just as bad inside as out, and that if the ancestors could pull off a show like this, then they probably had like thermal sensors or something that could image the bad kids hiding in the igloo or tent or cabin. Which made him think of the man Pierre.

He was bad. He had tried to kill them in all earnestness twice now. Once in dumping food and gear, once in brazen ambush. It boggled his mind that Wynn still reserved a final judgment. What was he waiting for? To get shot? Even then he might plead terror on the man's behalf, he might insist that the man was convinced that *they*, Wynn and Jack, had abducted his wife.

Those ancestors up there, they knew. They were looking down on the man tonight, too, Jack had no doubt, and if they wanted to enact punishment, and if Jack was the instrument of their vengeance, he was glad to oblige. Fuck Pierre. He would put a bullet in him in happy reciprocity, and if he didn't kill the man he'd be happy to truss him up like a calf at branding and tow him down the river on a log raft awash with waves. Happy to dump him before the elders or council or selectmen or whatever they were in Wapahk, where it sounded as if they might or might not call the Canadian Mounties. Tundra justice. Wife-killer. What was the word? Wynn had taken a single Latin class, he'd have to ask him.

Jack shrugged the rifle off his shoulder and took it in both hands and surveyed the camp. The fire: a nexus of vulnerability, a target, as conspicuous as a bull's-eye. The woman sleeping there. From here he could see the top of the wool hat, the red tassel, the outer sleeping bag moving steadily with her breath. Good. Off a ways, in the shifting light of the flames, the blue tent. At least it wasn't yellow. Wynn inside it. He knew his buddy—he'd be sleeping like the dead. Scratch that, bite your tongue: like a log, like an angel. Jack felt himself smile. Wynn was an angel in a way. He slept usually as soon as his head hit the pillow or rolled-up jacket, he slept easily and hard because, Jack figured, his conscience was clear and he had faith in the essential goodness of the universe and so felt cradled by it.

Imagine. That's what Jack thought. Imagine feeling that way. Like God held you in the palm of his hand or whatever. Wynn could take all the philosophy courses he wanted, and he had taken a few, and he could read the arguments of Kant, the treatises of Schopenhauer and Nietzsche, and he did, and he got really excited about them, tried to explain them to Jack, but in the end, though he did not think of himself as religious in the least, Wynn would bet all his chips on goodness. It wasn't even a bet, was it? It was no decision at all. Like the fish who had no idea what water was: Wynn swam in it. The universe cradled him, it cradled all beings, everything would work out. Beings suffered, that sucked; *he* himself suffered, it certainly sucked; but step back far enough and take the long view and everything would take care of itself.

It sort of awed Jack. Sometimes, usually, it made him crazy.

He remembered visiting Wynn's family in Putney one time. It was last fall, the fall of their junior year. Wynn's little sister, Jess—who had clearly been a surprise to everyone, she was ten—followed them around. If they sat by the woodstove, she did, too. If Jack put in a dip, she demanded to try Skoal, and was so adamant that Jack opened the tin and said quietly, "Suit yourself. Best if you take that first one like the size of an ant." She didn't. She saw what he took and dug her fingers in and tucked it in her lip the way he showed her and she threw up and almost passed out. If they swapped jokes, she asked them what the Zero said to the Eight: "Nice belt!" She was such a tenacious pain in the ass that Jack couldn't help himself and became crazy fond of her. She was brilliant, too. She had read *The Hobbit* in three days. She had been born with cerebral palsy and had undergone a dozen operations to lengthen tendons, and now the only visible effect was that her right hand curled and she walked with a quad cane and a limp. Jack and Wynn had gotten up from a big lunch on a windy, sunlit Saturday, with the leaves of the maples blowing onto the trails, and announced that they were going to run up Putney Mountain. Jess announced that she wanted to go, and Wynn didn't hesitate. It awed Jack: Wynn said, "Put on your running shoes, let's go." He ran the two-mile climbing trail with Jess on his back, she laughing and chattering the whole way. When they got to the rocky top, which Wynn's cousin Geordie had cleared so that they could stand on granite and look across to Monadnock and over a little cliff to Brookline Road—when they got there and caught their breath, Wynn said that they had to make a sacrifice to the volcano and told Jack to take Jess's legs. Wynn took her arms and they swung her hard and high out over the cliff edge, counting down to the launch while she screamed and laughed hysterically.

They put her down. Jack had maybe never seen a person so happy. Wynn split up a Dairy Milk chocolate bar between them and told Jess that she really had nothing to worry about, they couldn't really throw her off until she was twelve.

Jack looked at the tent awash in firelight and thought that if that's the way Wynn saw, or felt, the world, then he was very lucky. Who was he to wish him otherwise?

He went back to the fire and put down the rifle and set his hand against the woman's throat and checked her pulse as Wynn had instructed. Steady and slow, not weak. Good. Food and rest could work wonders.

~

He nodded off. He jerked his head up and cursed himself and he wondered how long, and he saw the Milky Way and figured he'd been asleep two hours, maybe more. The northern lights lay against the northern horizon and they pulsed and flared like the lava inside a volcano and spread in pinks and purples; he had never heard they could become those colors. Still infinitely remote and silent, like something that wanted to be forgotten and never would be. What it seemed. He thought about waking Wynn and getting some serious sleep. If the man Pierre was going to attack he would have done so by now. Probably. It was probably about two, two thirty right now; the man might be waiting for the magic ambush hour of four a.m., the hour used by police and assassins and generals worldwide, the dead of night, insomniacs' bane, the Portal. He'd always thought of it that way: that there were portals in reality, in time and space, in geography, in seasons, when and where the dead or the very far away rubbed up against the living. It was in that hour or two before dawn, when the slip of ruddy moon was sinking like a lightship over the mesa at home, that he would hear his mother singing. That he would call to her and she would answer back in a voice as quiet as those lights.

A good time to attack because in that hour, if someone was not asleep, he was probably transported by longing as Jack was, and in some way asking to be taken. He would not be that person. He would not let Wynn be. He wished almost more than anything right then that they had some coffee, but they didn't. A shirr and flutter in the darkness zinged him wide awake, but it was just a small flock tumbling past as if windblown. Just over the tops of the living trees.

CHAPTER FOURTEEN

At dawn, before sunup, Jack woke Wynn and they broke what there was of camp, not much, and portaged the canoe to the small shale beach below the big rapid where Jack had last seen the man. They took time and care to douse the embers of their fire with water carried in the pot, though they thought, but did not say, that it was a little like stacking a line of sandbags before a tsunami. Well. With everything seeming to fall apart, good habits were one thing to hold on to.

Wynn asked Jack if his stomach was cramping up as his was and Jack said yes. Too many blueberries and nothing else. They had only five dried meals left and they were saving them for her. On the map there was a creek entering the river just around the corner. They would stop and make a breakfast camp and fish. Wynn carried the woman this time in his arms and they loaded her without waking her, which was either a good or a bad sign, and they shoved off.

No sign of the man. Good. He had not made camp at the obvious spot below the rapid, by the first creek, he had forsworn the clear water and sandy flat for distance. Good. They had made a bed for her in the boat from fir branches and they lifted her off it and laid her on an inflated Therm-a-Rest on the sand. She was breathing steadily and she was warm inside the two sleeping bags, so they left her. Before they moved her again they might ask her to drink something, maybe sweet water.

They slipped the rods from the tubes and jointed them and strung the lines and began to fish. It was a small creek, running shallow over sand at the mouth and narrowing to a channel the color of black tea where it emerged from the trees. They smelled smoke only now and then, but when the wind was right it was strong and rank. They fished without joy now. They knew they were beginning to starve. There was no hatch of insects that they could see, which was odd on a sun-warmed morning, and no pupae on the rocks of the bed. Maybe the water was too acidic, they didn't know, but they picked the flies with more care; they did not confer but reached into their own archives of past summer mornings on slow tannin creeks. Jack had been kept company in the night by a single cold cricket so he tied on a small hopper. He hit the leaves and stems of the grass and asters along the bank and let the hopper bounce off them and fall in like a wayward jump. Wynn used a little wooly bugger which he stripped upstream to mimic a fry or minnow. They began catching fish and they relaxed, and they kept every trout now that was bigger than their clip knives, everything that could offer a couple of bites. In less than an hour they had a panful, and they rustled together a fire and cleaned the fish.

They steamed the brookies in an inch of water in the pot and wondered why they hadn't thought to pack salt in the emergency box. Jack said, "Ten each? To start?" and they dug in. They speared each fish with their knives and at first laid it in their palms and unzipped the spine with its rows of needled bones. After a few they figured out how to dangle the small fish by the tail and strip the meat off the bones with their teeth. They started slowly and picked up speed. The first few hit their stomachs and it was only then they knew they were ravenous for protein, and they felt nauseous at the same time, which was novel. They were spitting errant bones into the fire and when they finished ten Jack counted and said, "Seven more," and they finished them. They felt logy and bloated and Wynn gagged but managed to keep the food down, and they grabbed the rods and fished for another hour and made themselves eat again. They didn't care if it took most of the morning. This time they tried making a grill of willow saplings and roasting the brookies over the coals but found they lost too much of the skin when it burned, so they went back to steaming. They ate another round. They lay back against the rocks groaning and looked at each other, sated and miserable, and Jack said, "You better not fucking throw up. I'm sick of fishing this morning." And they started laughing so hard they almost did barf. Relief. Just the laughter. It was like a warm rain. A rain that would tamp and douse the forest fire and rinse away the sweat and the fear.

~

They did bathe. Before they launched again they stripped and rolled in the shallow water of the brook. It was dark but clear like brown glass and so cold they gasped.

They lay back on the rocks in the sun and let it dry them. Wynn liked to lay one cheek and then the other against a warm smooth stone and smell the mineral heat. A downstream wind poured over their wet skin and raised goosebumps. If one concentrated on one thing and then another—the good things in each moment—the fear wrapped deep in the gut seemed to unswell, like an iced bruise. Still there, but quieter.

As they lay drying, Jack said he understood now how Canadian trappers who had tried to survive through the winter on flour and rabbits had died. Starved for fat. It's what he craved now. The ones in the camps who made doughnuts in lard lived. He'd give his frigging right arm for a doughnut. A Krispy Kreme glazed in sugar floated across his mind like an angel. It scared him, because they'd barely made a day and had at least a week to go.

But they could live on berries and trout for a week, no problem. Had they been at their leisure it would have been fun to forage every day, to fish for food.

When they were dry and dressed, they sat her up and Wynn held her against him and Jack asked her gently to wake up and eat a little. Drink. She did. They made another of the packet meals—they'd had five left, now four—beef stroganoff, and Jack spooned it into her and she ate half. She chewed slowly, as if in pain, and at one point her eyes flickered open and she saw them. She saw them. Her greenish eyes blurred over Jack, then focused. "Where?" she rasped. "The other?"

"He's holding you up, ma'am," Jack said. "Hold on." Jack grasped one side of the sleeping bag and Wynn shifted from behind her and came around to the front, his arm still around her shoulders. She looked from one to the other. It took great effort. "Thank you," she whispered. "Both." Her eyes closed again and she drifted off. They carried her to the canoe and laid her on the bed of boughs. Jack levered the rifle to open the breech and checked one more time that a cartridge was chambered, and they shoved off.

~

The day was half gone. They paddled steadily without letup. The wind shifted around to the west and for the first time they could see the hazy thickening of air that was not yet rolling smoke and the birds in flocks that were smaller now, and many single birds, mostly duller-colored, the females, and Wynn posited that these were the mother birds with hatchlings who had refused to leave their nests until just before the flames. That was heartbreaking if you thought about it.

The cadence of the paddle strokes was high and it hurt after a couple of hours and so they weren't thinking about a lot. Jack had pored over the map and there would be a few riffles and smaller rapids and nothing to portage for two days, so he was at a loss as to where to expect the next attack. They had passed a wide cove with a pair of loons, one was probably nested nearby, and when they stroked past, the one closest tilted back her head and loosed a pitched wail that must have moved the trees like wind. It pierced the haze and echoed off the waiting forest and rolled over the water like any scream, and seemed to carry a pathos so deep it was a wonder a mere world could support it. Maybe she knew what was coming. Maybe she had hatchlings in a nest and nowhere to go and she knew.

Others did. Because now as they paddled into the afternoon they saw the first moose. Two. A big female with a calf. The moose trotted to the open margin of the left riverbank and clattered over the broken shale on stiff legs and entered the water without pause, and she stretched her neck and let the water sweep her without concern and set a ferry angle and swam across. The calf mimicked the mother. They could hear the chuffs of their breathing. They were only yards ahead of them. The next was a bull moose, and then a black bear with two cubs. The cubs hesitated at water's edge, they seemed frightened, and the mama bear snorted and waded out of the river and got behind them and drove them forward. They swam. The littler one lost ground in the current and Wynn thought he would get swept away, but the mother got below him and bumped and shouldered and goaded him across. Damn. They could hear the other cub, who had reached the far bank first, bawling and bawling. They saw mink cross, and squirrels. In late afternoon Jack had his head down, paddling hard, trying to maintain the tempo, and Wynn whistled and he looked up and saw what must have been a hundred mice. They'd never heard of such a thing. It was like a miniature herd. They swarmed a steep cut bank and fell or jumped or dripped off it into the water and they swam. Who knew how they kept track of the correct direction, but they did. They came across the current in a moil.

"Looks like Dunkirk," Jack said.

"Fucking A."

They saw woodland caribou, a small herd of bulls at first, three smaller and two with massive racks, who took to the river as the moose did, with zero hesitation. Toward the end of the afternoon they both sang out as one: they came down through a riffle of small waves and ahead was an entire string of caribou swimming the river in single file. They counted twenty-three. Jesus. Later Jack wondered why they hadn't thought to shoot one for meat and could only think that they'd been smitten with awe. They had never seen anything like it.

And they could see smoke now. Real smoke. It was gray, not black, and it did not plume but hazed west to east across the river as the animals had done. Still they could not hear a thing but wind and their own paddles, and the river listing along the rocks of the banks and sifting in the deadfalls.

They paddled into the dusk because they could. They stuck to the middle of the river so as to be less of a target from either side. Jack did not think Pierre was a crack shot—just a feeling. They were drifting now, taking a break and drinking, tossing the filter bottle back and forth. They must both have been thinking the same thing, because Wynn said, "I feel pretty safe out here. In the middle. Maybe I shouldn't."

Jack said, "From the fire or the man?"

"The man."

Jack squeezed the last of the bottle, dipped it over the side and refilled it, tossed it back.

"Well, he's not a hunter. There's that." Jack scanned the banks.

"No?" Wynn said. He looked uneasily along the shore.

"Nope. Did you see him when he first came around the corner the other day?"

"Yeah." It was a question.

"He was staring straight ahead. Looking for the lip of the falls. Fixated on it."

"Yeah . . . So?"

"A hunter would've been scanning the shore. It's instinct. Even you would have done it."

"Fuck you. You want more?" Wynn held up the bottle.

"Nah, I'm good. I'm serious. Even with a major drop coming up. I've watched you. As long as he's in flat water, a hunter'll be scanning the shore. For sign like the breaks of game trails. For movement. For shapes, shifts at the edges of shadows, color. Can't help himself. Pierre, he didn't do any of that. That's instinct. This fucker fixated on the single danger downstream. And he still almost missed the portage. He can paddle okay, we saw him ferry across, but he's bush league."

Wynn almost laughed. That Jack could judge a man's character in two seconds, at two hundred yards.

"That's reason for optimism, right?" Wynn said.

"Take it where you can get it."

~

They paddled on, looking now for a place to camp. The filter bottle was getting harder and harder to squeeze—the filter was clogging up with dirt from the river. They'd try to nurse it. From what they could judge of where they might be on the map, there were no tributary brooks forthcoming, so they'd have to boil water out of the river. They'd sterilize a potful and let the sediment settle out of it before they drank it. When they did get to a clearer creek, Wynn would try to clean out the filter again. They also had the iodine in the day box—they could use it to purify water if they had to.

The river flowed between walls of black timber here, which thickened the twilight. They could smell the spruce, the cold tang of them, as if they were exhaling at the end of a long day. Soon the first stars burned through the haze and the temperature was dropping, but it was still light enough to see. They were paddling slowly, scanning for a clearing, a good take-out, and Jack held up a hand. "Look," he said.

Something was swimming ahead of them: it was a caribou calf. They saw no cow, just the little calf trying to keep itself afloat. The stiff current between the narrow banks was getting the best of her and she was twisting her head in panic. Jack waved Wynn forward and they picked up the pace. Jack looked to the left bank and upriver: no sign of a mother. Wynn guided them with precision and slid the bow just behind the thrashing calf, whose breath blew fast and panicky. Wynn slid the bow so she was on the right side and Jack scooped an arm in water and hauled up the kicking caribou. Her slicked fur was tawny, her nose almost black, and she was rib thin, Jack could feel them beneath the warm hide of her chest. Still nursing. Without a mother at the leading edge of the fire she was doomed. He glanced at Wynn. Wynn had never seen that face—it was raw grief. Jack was struggling with the thrashing calf and for just a moment the hard set of his face fell away and Wynn saw a kid stricken and not willing to accept any of this. Wynn nodded, *Okay. Okay.* And in a flash Jack's right hand went to the clip knife in his pocket and in a flash thumbed it open and at the same time his left arm gripped the calf's head tight and twisted it back and he plunged the knife in her tightened throat and ripped upward and she uttered a sound like a startled bird and the kicking quieted and she bled and was gone.

They drifted. Wynn had looked away and when he looked back Jack had the little caribou across his lap, he was bent over her letting the blood run freely over his legs and Wynn could not see his face.

~

They could no longer camp on the left shore. It would be crazy with the fire coming who knew when. But the river was too narrow here and neither harbored any hope that the right bank would offer further protection. Forty yards was wide but it wasn't enough. If the fire came and there was any wind at all it would jump. In nine or ten miles, according to the map, the banks widened out a little, but the river was dropping here, off the edge of the Canadian Shield, and it steepened just enough to kick up rapids and riffles, and neither wanted to broach on some rock and flip in the dark. They could feel another hard frost coming and neither wanted to get wet and freeze to death in the night. They'd had Farmer John wetsuits for whatever whitewater, but they'd been in the blue barrels, now gone, and anyway there were only two suits. Wynn couldn't help but think of Frost's poem "Fire and Ice," thinking of the first time he'd read it. He could picture his kitchen table back in Vermont. He had been so taken with the music of it, the near-nursery-rhyme

singsong juxtaposed to the clear-eyed . . . what? nihilism? he'd
read it to Jess.

Some say the world will end in fire,
Some say in ice.
From what I've tasted of desire
I hold with those who favor fire.
But if it had to perish twice,
I think I know enough of hate
To say that for destruction ice
Is also great
And would suffice.

Jess had pursed her lips, which she did when she was thinking
hard, and said, "How about flood? I thought it was supposed to
be flood." She was nine then, sharp as a tack. He'd never imagined that in a few short years he might have to choose between
freeze and burn.

They pulled over at a slab of bedrock close-backed by trees.
No choice. The granite sloped to the river in two overlapping
shelves. Jack hopped out and trotted to the edge of the woods
while Wynn held the canoe against the bank. Jack came back,
said, "There's thick moss. We'll put her in the tent tonight."

"No fire?"

"I dunno. Sucked last night. I don't wanna give Dickhead a
target again."

Wynn looked around at the leaning forest, the straight stretch
of river, which had darkened and silvered like a black mirror.
"Okay." Then he said, "What if it hits tonight?"

Jack didn't say anything. What was there to say? They could launch the canoe. They could wrap her in the sleeping bags and the emergency blanket and tent fly and themselves in their Gore-Tex raingear and douse everyone with water from the three-quart pot and paddle through it and pray. The water on the nylon would freeze tonight, he was sure of it. It didn't seem like a good plan.

"Do you wanna climb a tree and look?"

Jack didn't answer. He looked around them. His mouth was dry and for the first time he coughed. From the smoke. He'd studied the map that afternoon when they were drifting, catching their breath, and he knew that the country around them was flat. He could climb a tree, but he knew that unless he was on some rise, he would not see past the forest on the far bank. He might see thickening smoke but nothing else.

He said, "What's the point, Big? We—I—won't see past those trees. What can we do anyway? Tonight?"

"We could keep going."

"And navigate the rapids by sound?"

"We've done it before." Which was true. They'd taken a western river trip last summer and paddled out of the Gates of Lodore on the Green in the dark. Through Split Mountain Canyon. It was a rush and it was hair-raising.

"That was in kayaks. That's way different."

Wynn climbed out of the canoe and they both hauled it onto the bedrock. On some other night maybe, even a week before, they might have been more careful with the hull. Wynn might have winced at the grating of tiny pebbles as they dragged the boat up with the woman in it, but now he didn't. She jerked back and then forward against the dry bag like a child being hauled in a toboggan, and remarkably she sat up and looked around her.

"It's smoky," she croaked. Jack and Wynn glanced at each other. Her eyes were open. The swelling along the blades of her cheek was almost gone. She looked . . . like a normal person— disarrayed, half the hair loosed from her braid, dark circles of deep fatigue under her eyes, but blinking and alert.

"Are you in pain?" Wynn said.

She shook her head. "A little."

"Where?"

"Here." She motioned to the side of her head where he had sewed the gash. "And here." She touched her stomach.

"Sharp or dull?" He didn't know why he asked her that. He wasn't a doctor, what could he do with the information?

"Dull." She touched her head. "Sharp." She touched her stomach. Well, okay. Probably not an infection in the cut on her head—that would be sharp, wouldn't it? And who knew what in her gut.

"Do you have to pee?"

"God, yes."

They helped her stand. They held her while she stepped onto the rock. "I can walk," she said. She took a couple of tentative steps, swayed, held out an arm and Wynn grabbed it. She breathed and tried again, asked to be released, and they watched her walk uncertainly to the trees. They stood there. Neither knew what to do now. Should they screw the tactical worries and make camp? Make a fire? So they could roast the little caribou calf and all sleep comfortably? Two in the tent and one by the fire? And pray that whatever was coming held off until daylight, until they could maybe paddle through it, paddle the whitewater? Or pray that the thing never came at all, that it somehow died out or turned south, that the hardest rain of the summer would sweep in tonight? Fat chance. It was coming.

She came back. Slowly, a little drunk with weakness, but she came.

"Okay?" Wynn said. He couldn't hide his anxiety. "Thirsty?"

It took her a second to locate him. She was like a very old person, trying to keep all the parts together while she executed a simple task. Her eyes swept past him once and came back and settled on his face, like a frightened searchlight.

"Okay," she said. "I have blood in my stool." If they felt paralyzed standing there, her words did not help. Neither knew what to say. She sat down gingerly on a low ledge of the bedrock. She looked at the boys.

"I'm not dead," she said. "I don't think I am."

Jack set his cap back and rubbed his eyes and cheeks with the back of his hand. "Well," he said.

"We're going to get you out and to a hospital," Wynn said. It sounded lame. To him. Her lips quivered into a smile.

"Thank you," she said. That was it. That was all she seemed able to muster. Given the last few days, it seemed like a lot. Jack went to the canoe and pulled out the water bottle, which was half full, and took it to her, and she drank gratefully, eyes closed. He squatted beside her and when she opened them she found his face and let her eyes rove over it. They were jade-green with flecks of gold—or Kevlar. What Jack thought. And he saw them darken exactly as if a cloud shadow had passed over. Or the shadow of a huge bird. "Where's Pierre?" she said.

CHAPTER FIFTEEN

The question was flat but tinged with concern or fear. Jack was
less startled by the question than by her composure.

"Downstream," he said. Which was the simplest answer. She
nodded, grimaced.

"Data," she murmured.

"*What?*" Jack said.

"Does he have my data?"

Jack's jaw may have dropped. Wynn hovered over them like La
Tree and felt again like he was in a weird dream.

"*Data?*" Jack said.

She lifted her right hand in an attempt to wave it away. For a
moment they all held still, as in some incredulous tableau. Jack
said, "Did he do this to you?" It was the question he'd wanted

to ask for three days and he wasn't going to delay it while she lost consciousness again. He wanted Wynn to hear the answer.

Her brow furrowed. As if she were trying to remember. *Really?* Jack thought. *Are you kidding? We're not going to get a straight answer?*

"We were arguing," she said. "That morning with the thick fog and wind, I remember that."

"Yeah?" Wynn said, eager, from somewhere above.

"I was really mad. He was going back on his promise. That it was my trip." She looked from one to the other vaguely. Her voice was weak. Jack was afraid she would pass out. He put a hand on her good shoulder.

"Okay, your trip. What do you mean?"

"My study," she said. The words were faint. Uh-oh. But she was just straining to remember. It looked like it was causing her physical pain. "He would be *my* research assistant this time and it was *my* study."

"Okaaay," Jack said. "And?"

"And I was so mad. Wouldn't you be?" Jack felt lost at sea. He saw tears trickle from the corners of her eyes. At least she was cogent. Remarkably. She was like one of those coma patients you read about who wake up after months and start talking about their vacation plans.

"Yeah, sure," he said. "Then what?"

"I turned around and walked away. Fuck him, right?"

"Right. Fuck him."

"And he grabbed my arm really hard and spun me back."

Okay, the dislocation. They were getting somewhere.

"It was violent. It really hurt. I think he dislocated my shoulder."

"He did," Wynn said. She looked up at him as if seeing him for the first time.

"Oh," she said. "Yes." As if she'd forgotten what she was agree-ing to.

"That's why it's in a sling," Wynn suggested gently. "Jack popped it back in."

"Oh, thanks." She looked down at her arm in the sling. Almost as if it didn't belong to her but to someone else.

"Then what?" Jack said.

Her eyes found his face. "Then what what?" she said.

"After he grabbed you and hurt your arm."

"I don't know. I screamed at him. It really hurt. My arm hung there. I turned away. I was going to go to the canoe and find the phone and call Pickle Lake for a flight out. I was done. As far as I was concerned, the marriage was over. I told him." Her face remained placid but the tears ran.

Jack said, "You had a *phone?*" He thought how badly they could use it now, to call in a chopper, to get her out.

She nodded.

"Then what?"

"He was yelling that the marriage was not over, no way, and he grabbed me again and I spun back and hit him with my good hand. I slapped him, I guess, and I knocked his glasses off. They hit the rocks. Broke. His only pair. We just stared at them. He's pretty nearsighted."

"Nearsighted?" Jack said.

"He told me once that at forty feet he can see it's a dog but not what kind of dog."

A lot was coming clear: why the man had been straining to see the drop of the falls when he had come around the bend, why he hadn't chosen to ambush them at that first pullout but had tried at the second falls—because he didn't trust his vision and he needed them to be very close and tightly grouped. Where he'd been waiting on the ledge, the pullout was only twenty feet below him; they would have paddled right into the blast of his shotgun had Jack not made them take out above. Pierre could still paddle downstream, because running whitewater, he would see the blurred white of the big holes, enough to navigate around them. Damn.

"Then what?" Jack murmured.

"I said, 'Fuck you, serves you right,' and I walked away." Tears were streaming now.

"And?"

"I don't know. I blacked out."

Jack and Wynn looked at each other. Wynn cleared his throat. He was about to speak but thought better of it. Jack said, "What kind of study?" She blinked. "What kind of study were you two doing?"

"Buffering," she said. She closed her eyes and said sleepily, "The capacity of subarctic rivers and lakes to absorb acid rain. We're geochemists." She said it as if she'd said it a hundred times before. Which she probably had.

~

Jack skinned the calf quickly and boned her out, and they started a fire on the bedrock and roasted the backstraps first, which were the size of a summer sausage, then random cuts off the hindquarters. Surprisingly little meat, maybe twenty pounds. She had been a baby. They'd talked about the risk of the campfire, but it seemed the risk of being ambushed here, on a random bank, was much lower than the risks of gradually growing weaker. So they roasted the meat in strips draped across forked saplings and in skewered chunks and they all ate. The woman winced a few times as if the meat hitting her stomach caused her pain, but she kept tearing off small morsels and chewing slowly. They all badly wished they had some salt but no one spoke it. When they were done they boiled river water in the pot and made weak tea with one bag and added sugar. They had enough brown sugar for maybe two more pots. The tea and the protein and the calories revived them, Jack and Wynn. Her lids grew heavy and she nodded off. They fetched the sleeping bags and wrapped her and laid her on a Therm-a-Rest as they had before, and she slept. At their backs, away from the fire, the night was cold. In the swath of sky between the trees, the stars smoldered less through haze than through a screen of smoke. A clear night, and for the first time their eyes stung. At first they thought it was the smoke from their own fire, but the wind was carrying their sparks upstream. Jack coughed. Whatever it was chafed his throat.

They needed to paddle out of there in the cold and they did not have neoprene gloves and for the first time they said it out loud: they were fools.

"We're fools," Jack said.

Wynn was carving the knot of driftwood he'd found at the last lake camp. He cupped it tightly in his left hand and poked and worried the wood with the point of his clip knife as if he were using a chisel. "Why didn't we? Bring paddling gloves? Not much fabric for a whole lot of insurance."

"Because we're fools?"

"Right."

"Because we're minimalists. Which is a synonym for idiots."

"Right," Wynn said.

"Because you're a minimalist."

"Hold on a sec."

"I suggested we bring pogies, remember." They were tubes of neoprene that Velcroed around the paddle shafts like gauntlets and protected the hands. "And you said it was August." Wynn winced.

"What're you making?" Jack said.

Wynn shrugged. "Not sure."

Jack narrowed his eyes. "How do you work on something and not be sure?" He was razzing him. In truth, it was one of the things he admired about Wynn: how often he started a piece of art—with stones, with wood, even with paints—and had no idea.

Wynn looked up. "It's like cooking. You have a pile of ingredients and you start cooking and don't have a clue what you're making. Haven't you ever done that before?"

"No. Anyway, it's not like that. If you have a pile of ingredients and cook it it's going to be food. One way or another. That thing—it's a bird, or an elephant, or a boat. If you don't know what it is, how can you carve? You'll end up with a pile of shavings." That seemed to really bother Jack.

Wynn smiled. He held up a finger and said, "Ah, Grasshopper."

"Fuck you."

"You've been saying that a lot lately."

"I've been meaning it."

Wynn smiled and continued to carve whatever. He turned sideways a bit more to the fire to cast more light on the wood, and as he did the wind also shifted and blew the smoke crossways into the trees and they heard the surf. Crashing surf far off, buffeted and torn by wind. They both sat up, turned their heads. The surf surged and sifted back like breathing. They listened hard and could hear that it was punctuated with explosions like the crash of larger waves on rocks. And beneath it was a groan. A deep groan at a frequency lower almost than their ears could register, like something geologic. Like layers of bedrock rumbling over each other.

"Holy fuck," Jack whispered.

They could still see nothing, no change in the pallor of the night, which seemed, now that they stared, faintly illuminated by more than starlight. Maybe not. And then they heard a crack. Out of the roar of distant waves a shot like the spar of a giant ship breaking.

Jack cocked his ears as if he were receiving some alien broadcast. "The big ones," he said, "they talk. That's what my cousin said, the hotshot firefighter in Idaho."

"Talk?"

"The biggest fires. They talk, just like this. Listen."

They listened. Who knew how far off. Not close enough yet to crown the wall of woods with light. There were other sounds: turbines and the sudden shear of a strafing plane, a thousand thumping hooves in cavalcade, the clamor and thud of shields clashing, the swelling applause of multitudes drowned out as if by gusts of rain. Rain. Downpours. Washing through a valley and funneling over a pass. Crackling through woods and sodding over the tundra. Wynn closed his eyes and could swear he heard the sweep of a coming rainstorm. As if the fire in its fury could speak in tongues, could speak the language of every enemy. And sing, too. Over the rush, very faint, was a high-pitched thrum, a humming of air that rose and fell almost in melody.

Wynn walked to the water. He peered into the dark. Between the tall trees on either bank was a swath of stars, a river of constellations that flowed heedless and unperturbed. Between the brightest, needling the arm of Orion and the head of the Bull, were distances of fainter stars that formed, as Wynn stared, a deep current, uninterrupted, as infused with bubbles of light as the aerated water of a rapid. Except that he could see into it and through it and it held fathomless dimensions that were as void of emotion as they were infinite. And if that river flowed, that firmament, it flowed with a majestic stillness. Nothing had ever been so still. Could spirit live there? In such a cold and silent purity of distance? Maybe it wasn't silent at all. Maybe in the fires that consumed those stars were decibeled cyclones and trumpets and applause.

As in our own. Our very own voluble fire.

He looked straight across at the wall of trees: dark. A solid reassuring darkness. Not that reassuring. The rolling pops of trucks dumping gravel, the cracks of artillery, they were unnerving. How could they not see it? How could the sound travel and not the light?

What they didn't realize is that it had. It had traveled. The entire sky was so suffused with firelight that the billion stars were as faint as they would have been under the dominion of the fullest moon.

~

Which had not yet risen.

Wynn walked back.

"We're sitting ducks. Here. It's too narrow. The fire'll jump the river in a flash." He sat next to Jack by the campfire. "All those animals. Those single birds. Nest-sitters, right? The last to leave."

"What I was thinking."

"What do you want to do?"

Jack said, "Seems like if we just sit here, we'll die."

They listened. The measly pops of their campfire seemed to be puling to the greater roar. Jack said, "Like falling asleep in the snow. Feels like that. Like if we camp, it'll come."

Wynn said, "I was looking at the map. The river must've changed a lot since they surveyed it. It's been wider where I thought it'd be narrow, and there's those wide coves that aren't on the map."

"Nineteen fifty-nine. Says beneath the legend. The survey's sixty years old."

"Rivers change every year. Maybe—"

"Don't count on it. We'd need half a mile of river to even stand a chance of staying out of the fire."

"Yeah."

Jack said, "Lemme see what you've been carving."

Wynn worked three fingers into the pocket of his work pants and pulled out the chunk of wood and handed it to Jack. Just small enough to fit in the palm: a canoe. What else. The exact shape of their own—the exaggerated beam dead center, the sharply tapered bow and stern, the faintest rocker along her length. He had just begun carving out the shell—the outlines of the seats and thwarts were there in bare relief. Jack ran his fingers over the whittled planes of the hull and the pads of his fingertips seemed to relish the coarse rendering, the snags and chiseled edges. He handed it back.

"Is it a sex toy?"

"Fuck off."

"What do you want to do?"

"Do we have a choice?"

"No." Jack pulled out his tin of Skoal and took a sizable dip. It's what he often did when they were about to put in. He spat in the fire. "Ready?"

Jack walked over the stepped rock to the boat and began strapping stuff down as tight as he could while Wynn gently woke her up.

CHAPTER SIXTEEN

This time they all three wore the life vests. They put her in Jack's rain jacket and added more boughs to her seat to try to keep her out of the bilge water, but once they got into any kind of real rapids or even a feisty riffle she would get soaked. Not ideal, but then there was everything about the night that was not ideal. They did not bother dousing their fire: a tip of the hat, almost an acknowledgment of respect to the coming onslaught. They helped her into the canoe and launched. This time, without discussing it, they both got low. They were both on their knees, butts against the edge of the seats, and they picked up their paddles and stroked easily upstream to the top of the eddy and out into the main current and let the river send the bow around in a wide accelerating peel-out, and then they were heading downstream, paddling in tandem, steady, not fast, and they stared ahead intently at the unbroken surface until it seemed their eyes ached, and listened hard for a rush and sift that was of water not fire. The river between the phalanxed woods, the black bulwarks of forest, was something metallic, faintly luminous, and they each wished it would stay that way and knew that it wouldn't.

~

The cracks were the scariest. The sounds with no apparent flames. They paddled through an *S*-turn to staggered gunshots grown closer like an advancing front, which were the bigger trees exploding, and almost immediately they hit a long rapid. They could see the whitewater ahead like the thin line of distant surf, but it was much closer than it seemed and before they could scout a line or intuit one they each felt the waft of cold air and the rush came with it and the bow rocked up into a breaking wave and Jack braced the blade of his paddle into the froth and they were in it. Smack in the middle of the whitewater. They took water over the right side in the first wave but not much, but when they hit the second they took more, the gunwale gulped and she was awash in a couple of inches of ice water. They were heading left, they accelerated. They'd both seen and heard the gnash of a large hydraulic almost straight off the bow, a cresting pale hump that thumped and hissed in a lower register—the trough would be behind it—and they sprinted now, both, Wynn setting the left angle, not in unison, each paddling madly for enough speed to make it past the sucking hole. Wynn thought of nothing but speed, but he watched, amazed, as Maia reached for the cookpot clipped to the strap of the dry bag behind her and freed it and began to bail. She scooped and threw water over the side with her one good arm, with almost professional speed. Damn.

The stern just cleared it. The current accelerated at the left edge of the hydraulic and Wynn ruddered hard off the right side to straighten the boat and swing the stern away and around and even in the dark he looked down into a deep gnashing trough. They were in what they knew to be a ramping rock garden whelmed with whitewater, and the rush was so loud it went silent and they braced to hit a sleeper, the thud of a boulder barely underwater, and the sudden sideways upending, the flip and maybe the awful crunch of Kevlar as the boat wrapped and buckled around the rock . . .

And then they were by. The fast current and chop funneled down the middle of the river and the gradient seemed to level and they knew without looking that they were in a wave train, a rolling succession of breaking haystacks, and they did look and they could see the pale froth at the tops of the standing crests like whitecaps, and the crashing of water diminished to the discreet song of each single wave, and then the waves were smooth rollers, and then they were released: into the calm flat water of the pool, the metallic sheen of river stretching ahead again, almost placid, an uncertain respite.

She had bailed. Throughout the length of the rapid, and she bailed with one arm now as the current spun them into the flat. Must be feeling a lot better, Jack thought. He turned and said, "Phew." Loud enough they both could hear. Then: "Hand me the bailer, would ya?" She did. He reached for the soaked shirt stuffed with blueberries and untied a sleeve and funneled the pot full and handed it back. "Fuel," he said. "We might need it for the next one."

~

They let themselves drift, for now. Tugged northward. On their left rose a continuous muffled roar as of storm and turbines punctuated by the pitched whine and pops of pressure cookers as they explode. Nothing to see, still, but a thickening haze.

Jack thought it was eerie—the chorus of harsh instruments that should never commingle—and every now and then rose a thin scream exactly like someone being squeezed to death. Squeezed and sizzled to a last tortured hiss and then maybe the crack of a spirit being loosed to the heavens. It was terrible. The wind had backed west-northwest and it brought the bedlam along with rolling smoke that stung their eyes and made them cough. The water was swift and flat for now, at least there was that. Without talking the two picked up their paddles and began pulling the boat forward.

In the last couple of miles the river had widened, it was maybe a hundred and fifty yards across, and almost instinctually they hugged the right bank, away from the fire. Their hands were stiff with cold. Motionless tall trees on either side, still dense with darkness, except over the left treetops now fluttered a glow not bright but bright enough to erase the lowest tiers of stars. Jack held up his hand and Wynn rested. They listened. The jet roar was no longer muffled but rose and fell as if buffeted. Almost as if breathing.

Their throats burned. Jack almost had to yell. "It should lay down at night, but it's not. That's weird. It's plenty cold."

They drifted. Jack said, "If anything, the wind is stiffer."

They waited. Both knew he wasn't done, and both sensed he himself wasn't sure what he wanted to say. That was almost scarier than the sense of a mega-giant beast thumping closer beyond the wall of trees. Wynn thought of *Jurassic Park*. He said, "What rough beast . . . ?"

"What?"

"Nothing."

"It happens," Jack called. "A fire disobeys every rule. Anyway, it's close. No sparks yet or flying shit, there's that." Pause. Then: "The river isn't wide enough."

He'd said it. With a fire this big, the river wouldn't act as a fire-break. Nobody had to ask what he meant.

"You can hear it. It's just big as shit, the biggest fucking forest fire on earth. Right now that's a fact." He shook his head, trying to clear it maybe of the truth. "So it's coming across and the heat makes these crazy swirling gusts and it'll make its own weather. Little cyclones and windstorms. That's maybe the gusts we're feeling now. The head of it. The smoke will get thicker and that's gas and it'll roll across the river and if it ignites . . . well."

"We're toast."

"It's a flashover. But."

"But what?"

"I dunno." Jack had to make himself breathe steadily. He coughed. "I dunno. You know how sometimes a fire runs over some neighborhood and half a block of houses'll burn and then there'll be two that stand untouched, and then another block burned down to cinders?"

"Yeah?"

"It's uneven. It's not predictable. That's all I'm saying."

Wynn lifted his voice. "You're saying we better be those two houses."

~

The smoke did thicken. They hugged the right bank, the main current just along the eddy lines close to shore, and the smoke rolled, so dense the black mirror of the river ahead was clouded as in fog, and then the wind picked up and the smoke was peppered with flying sparks. Sparks first, then shreds like leaves but embered and glowing, then torn rags of bark laced with fire. Wynn thought of strips of burning skin. They flew across in the smoke and they spread and folded and tumbled as they blew and the boat plowed through them. Over the trees—they could still see the wall of trees through smoke like fog—the glow was a fierce and general radiance that pulsed with a redder breathing. It was loud. Whatever turbines roared were just beyond the trees and now they were cut by a sudden whoosh and pop, and then the terrible hissing squeal that Jack knew was a tree's sap, its lifeblood boiling and pressurized and squeezed through the very pores of the wood.

The sparks and flying tatters were hitting their backs and shoulders now. Wynn dumped the blueberries out of the pot and yelled at Maia to pull up her hood, she did, and he dipped the pan and doused her with water and then himself and he yelled and tossed the pot to Jack.

They needed to get to the bank. It was low along here, it was the shadow of a wall, a cut bank running to three or four feet above the water, running down to water's edge and rising again like a moldering stone fence. The fire was coming fast and they needed to get against the dirt down low maybe in the water and get their heads in moss or roots, he didn't know what. As he thought that, he heard another rush beneath the fire: the current was picking up. Holy fuck. The current was gathering speed, and the rush he was hearing had a wholly different key, something whiter, ancient, a violent register but now of water—it too was growing in strength, they were being sucked into the V'd current of another rapid. Jack peered into and through the smoke and flying debris—there were small sticks flying, burning sticks, that couldn't be good, some not that small—and he could barely see and feel that they were ramping into a rapid and it was a left-hand bend. Fuckin' A, at least that. A left-turning bend would pull the current to the outside of the turn, to the right bank, away from the blaze. At least that. Jack yelled, *"Rapid!"*

They grabbed paddles and stroked into the first breaking waves.

All they could do was keep it straight. Let the river pull them to the outside, right, and keep the canoe straight to the current, parallel, so anything they hit they'd hit dead on. Less chance of a flip. Not much to do, but something. They paddled and the first waves lapped over, and in the rolling plumes they strained to see the dark surface—it was broken by pale crashings but not everywhere, they needed to stay out of the holes. They were being sucked to the right, to the turning bank, and the bow reared and bucked and crashed down and they took on more water and she was bailing and if someone, anyone, was yelling they didn't hear it, it was subsumed in the general roar. And then the burst, ballistic, of a tree exploding, and beyond the scrim of trees, which was only a scrim now, the spruce were backlit and spindled as if by molten sun; beyond them, over the tops, they saw a jet of fire erupt skyward and heard the whoosh and saw a white billow as of steam against a sky no longer dark and then a whoosh and another tree exploded and the tops of the trees along the bank began to burn. It was crowning. Maybe it was awe. The awe of the earth burning to cinders— they could not not look and they missed seeing the hole and the bow reared and plunged into a deep backward-crashing trough. The stem of the canoe half reared again, wildly, claw-ing out of it, and the seething backwash flung them sideways and it was all water. Water pummeling, the roar gone strangely mute, and Jack tried to grab the boat, any piece of it, and was torn free, he held to the paddle and was shoved and beaten to the bottom. What a hole does: takes you under. Maybe it was deep but his knee struck stone and he was tumbling, knew he was free of the hydraulic, had the paddle, he buoyed up burst-ing for breath and came clear into a chop of boiling waves but no boulders, good, and the first thing he saw was the trees all along the riverbank catching fire, crown to crown.

Jack was swimming. He looked wildly around and saw that the canoe was right there, capsized and awash a few feet off. He lunged and threw an arm against the water-smooth hull and worked along it to the bow and found the rope. He grabbed it. He put the paddle in that hand and began kicking and swim-ming hard sidestroke, pulling the heavy boat behind him. Wynn saw it. He was just behind, had held to his paddle, too, the first reflex, and had been shoved to the bottom in the hole and came up thrashing for her and did not see her, and went

through a low crashing wave, and when he struck for the surface he came up against her. She was flailing with one arm and
choking and he yelled, screamed to flip on her back and she
did and he began hauling her hard to the right bank, following Jack. They all three were shoved down into the tailwater,
a long riffle, and they were very close to the bank, good, and
they got three, then four hard strokes past an outstuck boulder and were in the shore eddy which was wide and calm. No
calm for them. They buoyed into the narrow dark pool against
a shore of smoothed cobbles and Wynn was shoved against
Jack and felt the tug of Maia going past and he pulled her in,
and the canoe swung down below them against the bank and
Jack yelled, *"Get behind it! The boat!"* He gripped the bow rope
and now he let go of the paddle and pulled the shoulder of
Wynn's life vest, pulled the other two down into him—they
were in the shallows, maybe a foot, two, of ice water—and he
yanked the flipped canoe up to them and they all heard the
rush and saw the entire wall of trees across go to flame. The
thick smoke could not obscure it. They could feel the wind.
The wind was dense with sparks and flying debris. The canoe
was a low redoubt and they huddled behind it, the eddy current
keeping it straight to shore, and Jack screamed, *"It's crowning!*
Heads down, heads down! Faces down in the rocks!" They did.
They buried their faces between the cobbles in inches of water
and they felt a wind like some demonic thing, like nothing on
earth, a searing gust that pummeled the canoe, they could hear
the burning wood flail against it, the tick of embers, they were
lying in water heads down in the ice runnels between stones
and could not help but hear the passing over of hell.

It flashed over. There must have been a change of wind or one
measure of God's mercy. Because it did not bake them or sear
their lungs. Not a true flashover or they would be gone. But

they felt the hot gusts go over and then they heard the trees above them flare and scream like nothing human but spirit maybe, a singeing, crackling protest, and burning limbs began to break on the gravel bar. Also the wind stopped. The fierceness of it. As of a breath expelled. It was still there, pressing their backs, but no longer malign. Like a hot wind, like the ones that barrel up a desert river in late afternoon. Jack knew. He got to his knees and with one crazy heave he flipped the boat back over. Where was the pot? He'd clipped it to the thwart he was sure, he didn't see it, fuck it, the boat was awash but they were out of the rapids, the river was a mild riffle now, they had to get across. Back across. Back into the teeth of the burn. Because it was hot and flaming still but across the river it was already burned over, it was blackened, it had expelled its life and so all its ferocity. They had to get there because the head of the fire was on this side now and it was all waiting unburned fuel and it would flare, it was crowning above them, in a minute it would catch the whole bank and start creating its own wind as it had before, and if the wind backed around and the smoke and gases blew back over the water and flashed they could all still cook. The fire on this side could jump back over the river and there'd be nothing left to burn but them. He shook Wynn hard and his head came up and Jack said, "We've got to get back in the boat, now! When this whole bank really goes it can cook us, too. Now!" Wynn was dazed but nodded.

She was moaning. Good. She had not choked. Her injured arm had come free, lost the sling, it lay useless beside her. Wynn rolled her over and a burning twig hit her face; her face was wet, thank God, it hissed, he cursed and turned her on her side and said loudly in her ear, "Listen, we will rest soon, we've got to get back in the boat. Got to go now."

Wynn rose and turned and screamed. A burning mat struck the left side of his face. Jack spun. Leaf or bark in flame, and whipped where it fell by the back-gusting wind, it struck the side of Wynn's face and stuck like a burning hand and he slapped his palms to his cheek and screamed again and stumbled into thigh-deep water and fell in. Jack ran. Wynn was wallowing upward back onto the bank and he was cursing and trying not to touch his face where a raw strip exactly like the sear of a wide grill and curdled with blood cut his cheek from lip to the outside corner of his eye. Jack had grabbed him as he stumbled and Wynn stood and said, "I'm all right. It shocked me. I'm okay. Let's get the fuck out of here." He didn't look okay, but Jack thought, He has all his limbs, let's blow.

~

The canoe was awash, scraping rock—lucky it had not broken against a boulder. They left Maia where she lay and hauled the boat up on wet stones and under a rain of burning needles and branches managed to roll it and dump the water. The strapped bag and box and slung rifle had stayed in, thank God, but they'd lost the blueberries. There was the little steel pot swinging and knocking against the thwart. Wynn attacked the last few inches of water and bailed fast. Enough. The burning debris rained down, they swiped it off of arms, shoulders, and Jack had to hustle to Maia to kick a burning limb away from her leg—an inconstant blizzard of sparks, bunches of pine needles flaming like flares, birch leaves ignited to molten lace rained down, but the wind had gone quiet, it eddied as if confused, circled around them like a dog settling for sleep, the dense smoke had lightened, the jet roar had yielded to the crackling and shirr of a thousand campfires, it was eerie.

It scared Jack more than the full-on assault, he didn't know why. He did know: it was because the flash had burned through, the front line had stampeded past, they were just at the edge of a thousand square miles of new fuel ready to ignite, barely behind it, like standing at the tail of a T. rex. The fire was beginning to take hold in the new woods, it was beginning to crown in the tops of the new trees, they had to go. They slid the boat back into the shallows and carried Maia and shoved back into the smaller waves of the tailwater.

They did not look behind them now. They could hear again the gathering whispers, the swooshes and squeals, the cracks, almost as if the fire were questioning its own intentions and the woods were answering: "We have been waiting for you our whole lives." Less extreme violence now, more a difficult but cathartic conversation. That would change. Jack knew that soon the fire would rediscover its passion for death. They paddled. They did not ferry but angled downstream and across, and when they neared the far shore and Wynn began to turn her straight downstream Jack yelled, "Go to the bank!"

"What!"

"We're not safe on the river!"

Wynn was beyond questioning. In the wavering light from the burning behind them he saw on the left bank a country out of the *Inferno,* a shadowed world of stubs and spikes of blackened trunks still running with blue flame, or flaring, a ground charred to mineral dirt and scintillant with embers, and the bank itself was wholly strange: the exposed roots that ran over all these cut banks had burned and where they had embedded were now channels of blackened dirt like the remains of some horrible ant farm. He ruddered hard on the left and reset the angle and took them into a narrow gravel bar. Jack hopped out. He hauled the bow up on the rocks, which were strangely powdered with ash like snow and still hot.

"No rain," he called. "Not tonight. The river won't rise—we're safe leaving it."

"Leaving it?" Behind them two explosions. They did not turn to look, but the little beach was illuminated.

"Not safe," called Jack. "Not here." He did turn now to witness the new slaughter across the water: a straight stretch of river, how the fire was consuming the wall of trees in pockets that ran together, how different pieces surged and died. It reminded him of the aurora borealis he had seen the other night, the great forest beneath the stars seeming compelled to answer.

Wynn climbed out, glanced at Maia, she was awake, good, her eyes were wide and in them he could see a reflection of flames. He stepped up to Jack. On this side were only low hisses, a ticking and chirping, a simmering crackle like a million crickets, hellfire crickets, singing of apocalypse and char.

"What do you mean?" Wynn said. "Where do you think we should go?"

Jack pointed inland.

"There? Are you crazy?"

Jack took Wynn's shoulders and turned him around. The sections of fire all along the far bank were running together with increasing speed, and they could see the concatenate crownings as treetops burst into flame, see it quickening, the flames jetting higher.

"She will do again what she did on this side of the river," Jack said. "The fucker's getting hotter over there, she's just getting started. Once she makes her own weather she can do all sorts of crazy shit. Like back fully around. She can try to flash back. How wide is the river? A hundred thirty yards? It's not enough."

"Fuck." Wynn blew out the word. "Really? You really think so?"

Jack didn't answer. He let the spectacle across the water speak for itself. Finally he said, "Wildland firefighters call it running into the black. Back into the black. We won't run, not with her, but we need to go in there. It'll be uncomfortable but not so much as getting baked."

He let it sink in. Wynn nodded, but almost as if he believed he was in a bad dream now and it didn't matter what they did.

CHAPTER SEVENTEEN

Walking into the outskirts of hell is like: filling your rubber knee-high Wellingtons with an inch of water—just seemed like the right thing to do. He and Jack still had them, as Wynn had thought to shove them into the dry bag for the night paddle. In case. In case what happened happened. Had they been wearing them in the flip they would have lost them. So as they walked into the embered wasteland of a burned forest they sloshed with every step. Maybe because the moon was not up, and the light there was cast from exploding trees across the river—the sense again of pulse like blood or breath, like something alive. The scorched landscape throbbed with light. Otherwise black and red: black ground, black stumps, red embers, black distances between the flaring stumps. It was hot. They walked through charred spindles and spears—the simple skeletons of the old-growth trees. They wound around the hollowed broken rounds of trunks, some twenty feet tall, that speared the night and whispered with small flames that ran up and down the edges. They passed a stump sheared ragged at the top and still, incredibly, barked, if charred, and streaked with resin.

They passed one patch of spruce, maybe ten trees, singed but standing. How? Like retracing the tracks of fate. And if it was hellish at first, within a few minutes it felt holy. They held Maia upright between them to help her walk and they stepped slowly and nobody spoke. They avoided still-burning roots and feared those that burned beneath a layer of dirt. They sweated, and the ground was mostly very hot but it did not melt their boots more than a little. They coughed. Their sinuses burned but the smoke was mostly gone. They were aghast and awed. Nobody said a word but now and then one gasped.

They walked maybe a quarter mile and Jack whispered, "This is probably far enough. We'll just wait." His voice was a croak. He felt tired beyond reckoning. They scraped a patch of ash and scorched soil away with their boots and stood mute as the embered edges of the spiked trees breathed around them. It was not real. Jack looked around and thought that the *Inferno* was not credible: not because the details of Hell were beyond the pale—they were—but because of the unshakable equanimity of Virgil.

~

They waited there for hours. They leaned together and held her and slept like horses, standing. The ground was still too hot to sit on. She was weak and she buckled between them and they held her up. A crescent moon clawed out of the smoke to the east, a dim moon, heavy with blood. When she collapsed again they decided to move. It was too much—they'd take their chances on the beach.

They walked slowly back. They were dreamwalking now. She was mumbling, inarticulate. Jack couldn't look at Wynn; whenever they passed a stump still burning, the large sear on his face glistened with pus and blood. He kept his eyes on the retreating flames eastward, a dread stare, his arm gone numb from holding her up. Wynn held her belt and thought of nothing. He saw shadows passing, shaped like caribou, coyote, moose, fleet and weightless as smoke, he even saw a bear, and he knew they were ghosts. Or maybe his eyes were closed; he kept snapping them open.

They stumbled down the bank to the stony bar. The hulk of the canoe lay there unharmed and Jack startled with a jolt of adrenaline, the thought: What if the fire had flashed back and burned the boat? What would they have done then? No logs even to make a raft. He hadn't thought it through. They would have stood stunned on the narrow beach like castaways and watched a red sun rise on their own deaths.

Fuck. No way to truly reckon the odds, ever. They had been lucky. Was all this lucky?

They slept on the rocks, oblivious of the cold. At least the heat of the burn had dried their clothes and warmed their chilled bones. At the first touch of grainy light they slid the canoe to the water without a word and helped her in and she lay down against the bag and passed out. They shoved off and picked up the paddles. They could see their breath. In the gray dawn the river smoked with tendrils of mist. No wind, the water glass-smooth. No sound but the current frilling the stones of the bank. No bird chatter, no crickets. The river and the burns on either side were very still, the only movement there the tatters of flame worrying the biggest fallen logs. Jack said, "Big, we need fuel. Food. There won't be any berries for miles is my bet."

"Do you want to fish?" Thank God they'd broken down the rods and packed them in the bag.

"We'd better."

"Okay. I'll aim for the first creek." Wynn picked up his paddle and put it down again. The boat was still gliding from their first strokes—the silent slip and freedom from land like flight that they both so loved. "That was really close," he said.

"Yep."

"I feel relieved," Wynn said.

"Me, too. I do."

Wynn opened his mouth to speak, had nothing to say. Jack was half turned on the bow seat, watching him. "I know," Jack said. Wynn's face was torn open by the burn and smeared with black and runneled pale where the tears ran. "I know. We did good," Jack said. "We did." Jack felt his own tears spring and he turned in the seat and began to paddle.

~

It was exhaustion, Jack thought. The tears. Hunger, exposure, exhaustion. How long could they keep this up?

~

One good thing: the man would have no cover. Not up here. Had he survived the fire? He'd had maybe a day lead and might have missed it altogether. But then who knew how far down the river the fire ran? For all they knew it went to the delta, the coast. What would stop it? But they had to assume he still lived. In the burn they'd be able to see him way before they got into shotgun range. They still had the rifle, thank God. If the scope hadn't been knocked too badly they could drift and find him and pick their shot. Not they, Jack. Wynn would still not sanction the long-shot kill. Well, maybe he would now. Jack thought that it didn't matter—he would hunt and snipe the man the first chance, and as long as Wynn didn't fuck with him and try to unbalance the boat, he would kill him.

They paddled. The sun rose and burned almost crimson through the smoke that lay over the eastern horizon like a weather front, not even visible as sun until halfway to the zenith, and even then it was a hot red disk that looked more like some molten planet than a star. All along the cut banks were the scribed traces in damp earth where embedded roots had been, blackened and forking lines like some inscrutable calligraphy. The topography revealed was desolate. So much of the country had been covered in lichen and moss some-times feet thick, and it had all burned away in the night, and the underbrush, the fireweed and willows, all that was left was seared dirt and bedrock, the black spears of trees, sepul-chral, and without the woods there was the much longer view, the slight rising and falling of ground in every direction, the humps of eskers mostly bare of stumps, the folds where creeks had run, dry as if boiled off. Not fun, Wynn thought. The earth stripped to its geography did not feel like home.

There was still a handful of power bars in the day box and when Maia woke and sat up Wynn thumbed open the latches

and fished out three and they each ate one. They drifted. The
sugar in the blood felt almost like a cup of strong coffee and
each felt suddenly more awake, alert. They were starving, for
sure, Jack thought. He looked up and down the banks and of
course there was nothing, nothing to forage. And no wood, he
realized now, to make a fire. Though the thought of touching
match to wood almost made him shudder. They had the pot
still. How would they cook the last of the freeze-dried meals?
She could eat them soaked cold. How would they make tea
to fortify themselves? Forest fires were always, always patchy,
there would be spots along the bank that for whatever reason
had been jumped over, there had to be—they'd have to keep
their eyes out. For that, and for the man. Maybe it was the rush
of protein and sugar, but before he could take back the words
he spoke them: he said, "Maia. Maia, right? Your fucker husband was waiting in ambush back at the last falls. What are the
odds he will keep this up? I mean if he's not cinders by now."

He could see only the back of her head. The wild hair unbound
from the braid in the long swim. She'd also lost the wool hat
and the bandage. "You mean trying to kill us?" she said softly.
It surprised him. The ready, cogent answer. She must be heal-
ing somehow, even with all the trauma.

"Yes."

Jack glanced at Wynn, who looked stricken. Jack felt like slapping him. *What you don't want to look at can still kill you, Big.*
What he wanted to say but didn't. Well, he'd kill the man himself if it came to that.

She was very still. Not the stillness of passivity, but the stillness of holding oneself rigid in the face of some emotional

wind. She was definitely getting her strength back. "He tried to murder me."

"What I was thinking," Jack said gently.

She said, "Unless we are very lucky, someone is going to die."

~

They tried to make sense of the map. They had lost their bearings in the night paddle and were not sure which rapids they had passed. The river ran north but it meandered broadly, in places even bending south, and it had changed a lot since the survey in 1959, but the general contours must be the same. Still, it was hard to orient the map with the sun overhead. When it began to lower westward they'd have a better shot. Even better after dark. The last couple of nights had been clear, and tonight, with a long enough stretch of river visible ahead of them, they could probably get a bearing on the North Star and correlate the shape of the river they could see. It was important to put a pin in it. Jack said, "For one, we don't want to get surprised by another rapid. For two, he's operating under the same constraints: he can't let us pass him. So he'll be waiting again where he knows we'll stop, at the top of a portage. Right at the top of the next big drop."

Made sense. He might not find cover in the burned-over ground along the bank, but he might have it where the river erupted and fell—the biggest drops tend to be ledgy. As before. He could find plenty of cover behind rock outcrops. But. Anyway. They did not have to chase him. He would be waiting, surely. They needed food. The fire had been traumatic, but as they paddled steadily downstream on flat moving water they lamented even more the loss of the berries. It was a further violation: at the height of berry season, with the blueberries and blackberries and their cousins heavy on their stems and all the calories they'd probably need just at hand, the fire had thundered through and snatched it away. The river had taken care of the rest: in the flip they'd also lost the remainder of the caribou meat. It would have served them now.

Anything was better than nothing. After what must have been three miles of paddling through the burn, past huge toppled trunks still fluttering with yellow flame and pointed stumps sending up thin white smoke as if releasing the last of their spirits, they saw a creek entering in from river left. It flowed between low scorched banks and blackened stones, and it was scattered with fine ash but otherwise clear. They pulled out on the sand beach which seemed untouched, and they drank straight from the stream and pulled out their rods and strung them and began to fish. They figured if they caught any they could cook them over a still-burning stump. It lightened their spirits, enacting this simple routine, the steps of a ritual— piece together the rod, screw tight the locking ring against the reel, string the guides, pick a fly—the steps of a lifelong discipline that promised joy. They fished for an hour in the warmth of the afternoon—the freezing nights seemed to have cooled the days, too, it was no longer hot but pleasant and warm. They fished in the warm breeze and got not a single rise. No fry nor minnows darted past their ankles. As they cast and mended the lines and stripped them in, their moods sank. Neither wanted to be the first to say it. Wynn fished up to Jack and said, "They're gone."

"I know."

"It's shallow here. Do you think it could have boiled? Or all the ash?"

Jack shrugged.

"Why don't we see any floating?"

Jack shrugged. "I dunno. It flashed over. Twenty-five hundred degrees could boil a creek for sure. I just hadn't thought of it."

Wynn thought, You can't think of everything. And you're hard on yourself when you don't. Wynn would not shed tears again in front of his buddy, but somehow of all they had recently endured, the loss of the trout seemed the saddest.

They both heard it at the same time, a crunch behind them, of gravel, and they spun around and Maia was standing there. Her left arm cradled to her side, maybe covering some pain in her stomach. Disheveled, but standing.

"They didn't all die," she rasped. Her voice was almost normal. She seemed ... almost like a normal woman. "It happens. We—I've been in some big fires on our trips. My trips." She was snipping the man out of the snapshots, trying to. "They seem to know what's coming somehow and a lot of them will swim down into the river."

"No shit," Jack murmured. He was truly awed and relieved. The implacability and violence of nature always awed him. That it could be entirely heedless and yet so beautiful. That awed him. But also its intricate intelligence. Its balancings. Its quiet compensations. It was like some unnamed justice permeated everything. He would not go further than that. Still, the workings of nature made the voracious, self-satiating intelligence of humans seem of the lowest order, not the highest.

"They'll swim back up," she said. "By next summer, if the insects come back—and they will—so will many of the fish."

They all just stood there dumbly, in the sun and the smells of scalded earth, and the colder, welcome scents of the ashy creek, and absorbed the prospect of life returning. And the fact that they now had zero source of food.

~

They broke the rods down and stashed them back in the dry bag. They drank their fill of the creek, filled the battered, faithful pot full of clear water—the stream would not turn milky with mud and ash until the next rain—and they shoved off.

~

For a while they paddled slowly, then drifted. Without wind, in the middle of the current they were making four knots. They had not counted the tributary creeks they'd passed, nor reckoned their volume, but the streams were adding up and adding to the speed of the river. They were woozy with fatigue. With hunger. They did not have a plan. How many days were they from the village? They'd lost track.

Somewhere ahead they would know for sure. Because somewhere ahead was the biggest falls on the river, Last Chance, and from there they figured three days out. A few miles below the rapid was the confluence with the Pipestem, another big river that entered from the west, and after that the current would pick up, the two rivers together would widen, the gradient would flatten, and they could paddle everything then, every riffle. They could paddle it starving. They could drift it when the wind was down and save their strength. They would be home free. Probably. They did not have a plan, but neither did they plan on just letting the man shoot them.

Now the wind had quieted and they stroked slowly. Where the river ramped down around a bend and the current picked up they touched the water enough to keep the canoe straight and otherwise drifted. They knew: from here on out it was touch-and-go, they'd have to save their strength. And they'd have to stay awake and alert—they couldn't drift into the lethargy of the very hungry. When the man attacked they'd have to answer. Or attack first, which was apparently Jack's MO—who had known he had the temper of a killer? What Wynn was thinking as they drifted past a gravel bar on the right bank and an odd hump there, blackened and reeking like burned hair. He steered them closer in the easy current and they passed the stony flat within ten feet and he saw sticks jutting from the pile and the stench made him gag and then he realized it was a mother bear and cub, lying together and half burned, and he did gag and nothing came up.

"Jesus," Jack said. The cub was half under the mother as if seeking shelter, and in places the mama bear's hide was burned away and the fat beneath it too and the charry bones came through. They must have run just ahead of the juggernaut and made it across the river and been overcome with smoke and then it flashed over.

They drifted past and Jack said, "Hey, hey, wait a sec. Big. Pull over. We can salvage the meat."

"No way."

"We don't have a choice."

Wynn had gone ghost-white. He wiped his mouth on his forearm and his lips trembled and he took two strong strokes and let the current carry them past. This time he didn't listen to his friend. He was no way going to disturb the pair, and plus no meat from them would ever stay down.

Jack glared. Wynn did not apologize this time. He looked past his friend and paddled.

~

How long? Nobody kept track. The raw sun rose clear of the smoke and let a white sky rinse clean the blood. It tipped past its zenith. They paddled. It was not desultory, it was deliberate and slow. Nobody spoke. She slept. No more eagles as sentries flying down off the tops of the tallest trees, they were blackened spires standing along the banks like the masts of wrecked ships, and the fire had burned away the branches and the big nests. No more flycatchers chattering, no mergansers winging in pairs fast upstream, no more loons loosing their laughter and wails. Only the sift of current through the stubbed limbs of a burned and fallen pine, the occasional knock of a paddle, the sip of the dipping blades as they lifted out of water. At some time in the afternoon Wynn muttered, then called, "Fucking A."

"What?"

"Look."

Jack looked. On the right bank the burn ended. Or paused. It was like the border of another country. There was black waste-land and then there was green—willows, alders, the boister-ous fireweed flushing pink. And woods—the green-black of the spruce and fir, the rusty tamarack and yellowing birch. It was a miracle. What it felt like.

"Damn."

"It's a creek," Wynn said. It was. Wider than the ones they'd seen so far. The creek and the wind together had somehow conspired a hard edge. Pretty hard. A few of the taller trees in the green country had burned, but they had burned like torches in mostly solitary glory, and the boys could see that some had burned only partway, on one side, or in just the tops, and that the rest still lived. Wynn wondered if a tree had some analogy to pain. Or what pain would look like for a being with-out nerves.

"Should we see if there's fish?" he said.

"We'd better. Since we don't have any bear meat."

Wynn kept his mouth shut and set a harder J and paddled them in.

CHAPTER EIGHTEEN

Would a creek at the very edge boil? Would the fish on this side of the big river sense a fire and flee the way the others might have?

It was a blackwater creek like the others and scattered with white ash that must have drifted. In the eddies was a fine dust that filmed the water like pollen.

They saw no trout at first but strung the rods anyway. They were getting testy, they could feel reserves of goodwill sapping away. They needed to eat and they figured now, at least, if they got skunked with fish and protein they could scavenge for berries and consume enough calories to paddle out. A huge relief. They grounded the boat and Maia woke up and they hauled her higher onshore and unclipped the dry bag behind her and pulled out the rods. Wynn asked her if she needed help getting out or peeing or anything and she shook her head and the boys walked upstream a little and jointed their rods and began to fish. This time Wynn followed the brook into the divided country. His face throbbed and seared but it had gone dull and he could forget about it for minutes at a time. He needed a break from the river, and he needed a break from Jack. Also, he had never seen anything so oddly beautiful. The land rose gently away from the river eastward, there must have been some broad uplift beneath the soil, and so he could see the creek for a long way like some sinuous creature glinting in its scales and slithering down through the seam between the green and the black, life and death. The green side was feathery and unkempt, chaotic with being. The grass and brush along the bank, the flowers, limbs of the trees, all reached past each other for the light of the creek. He could hear warblers and thrushes. The black side was burned to soil; it had not much to say and was startlingly eloquent in its silence. Wynn thought the boundary was as stark and sad as Hades.

The wind rushed louder through the pines and moved the branches. His face felt as if a heated fork had been laid over his cheek, but as soon as he stepped into the water he forgot about it. He began to cast and the breeze pushed his fly, which was just a tuft of elk hair, toward the burn. He adjusted his cast and threw to the edge of the current. It felt very good to be alone with only the creek for company, the wind, the forest and the ghost of a forest on either side. He'd left his Wellingtons on the bank and waded up the sandy bottom on bare feet and the ice-cold water numbed his legs and he liked it.

He moved without thought. Flicked the caddis off the current and false-cast twice to dry the fly and let the loop overhead straighten and pointed his right thumb, which lay along the top of the cork handle, pointed it toward the center of the current with a straightening arm and let the wind push the fly south almost two feet and it landed on the seam, the wavering line between the eddy pooling along the shore and the push of flowing water, landed just an inch to the inside on moving current, right where he wanted the fly to be; it touched the silvered surface and began to bounce and bauble down toward him through the riffle. Perfect. He began to hum. Unconsciously at first and then he caught himself, it was one of the tunes that Jack sang, "Little Joe the Wrangler." He cast again, two feet farther upstream, where the eddy was darker and deeper, where a fish might be seeking more cover from kingfishers and eagles, and he thought what a sad tune it was, the little cowboy running his pony full-tilt in the storm, trying to turn the stampeding herd, and of course in streaks of lightning his buddies saw the horse stumble and fall. All the cowboy songs were like that. Pure, selfless souls who lived to ride the High Lonesome and sleep under the stars all meeting their pulpy ends under a thousand battering hooves. Or shot in the breast over some sweetheart who could never hope to match their goodness. Early death, that was the theme. The wages of innocence. Only the good die young. Why did Jack like those songs? Maybe because he knew he had enough badness in him to vouchsafe his future? An affirmation. He had certainly been acting differently lately. Like someone Wynn hardly knew. The ruthlessness. It scared him a little. But then, hadn't he always sensed it was there? Wasn't it part of what had drawn him to Jack in the first place?

His fly hit the water and was met with a small splash and tug. A hard tug, and Wynn's spirit leapt and the rod tip doubled and quivered and he felt the trembling through his hand and arm and, it seemed, straight to his heart, where it surged a strong dose of joy into his bloodstream. What a strange sensation, almost novel. It had been a while. He only realized then how long. How dour he, they, had become. Whatever. He had a fish on now, and not a tiny brookie, and not big enough either to bring in on the reel. He stripped the line in by hand and when the trout jerked hard and made a run he let the line slip back out through his fingers and gradually tightened the grip again as he felt the fish tire at the end of his sprint and he began again to pull him in. It was not a long fight and not a huge fish, but it was a fourteen-inch brown—who knew how they had come to live way up here—big enough, the first like him they'd seen, and with a gratitude and quiet joy he did not know he still had he got the slapping fish up on the rocks and thanked him simply and thwacked him on a smooth stone and the golden trout went still. Phew. Lunch. A few more like that and they'd be set for the day.

He did not call out. On another day he would have whistled or yelped. Especially on new water, or on water they weren't sure about. He almost did, but then he swallowed it. And it surprised him. He wanted to hold on to the quiet, the sense of being alone with the strange afternoon. Because it was strange. Being at this edge was like standing at the high-tide line of a tsunami. Looking out over the wreckage and death. The sense that you could turn around and walk away into the hills, and life.

It might not be that simple with a homicidal freak downstream, but for now the sun was shining and the day was warming and they would have fish for supper.

~

Jack caught trout, too. A handful of small brookies and a brown, not as big as Wynn's but a good part of a meal. They made a fire on the beach and steamed the fish in the pot. Maia was awake. She climbed out of the canoe unsure of her balance and walked unsteadily toward them, and they both stood quickly and went to help her.

She almost buckled as soon as they had her but she stayed on her feet and smiled a sad apology. Sadness or apology, it was the same. She had gotten them into this. "If it wasn't for me," she murmured, "you two would be long gone."

They lowered her to the stones where she could use a driftwood stump as a backrest. She smiled again and said, "Optimism. All that green and the end of the burn."

They split all the fish three ways and wished again they had salt and devoured it all. It didn't feel like enough but it felt better. They didn't see any berries here but knew they should find more farther down, so the stress of starvation seemed lifted for now. She ate, but she winced often and her skin was white and Wynn saw her press her stomach with her good arm as if she were quelling spasms.

Jack tossed a strip of fine bones into the coals. "He probably made it through," he said. "The fire. If this is the northern edge and he is ahead of us by a day, he made it through."

They both looked at him.

"Will he get harder or weaker?" Jack said.

Her eyes flickered. They were sleepy eyes, almost drugged. "What do you mean?"

"I mean will all the waiting and stalking make him sharper? Will it hone him or erode him? Will he start to waver?"

"He doesn't second-guess himself, if that's what you mean."

Jack nodded.

She grimaced, and Wynn thought it was either her injuries or the thought of her husband. She said, "He told me that when he applied to prep school in Connecticut, the admissions director asked him to name his best quality. 'I'm tenacious,' Pierre said. 'Okay,' the man said. 'What's your worst?' 'I'm stubborn,' he said."

"So Pierre's a psychopath and also cute."

She shrugged her good shoulder.

"Why does he want you dead so bad?"

"Because he tried to kill me and screwed up?"

"Yeah, I mean before."

"I'm starting to think it's for the same reason he married me." She half turned, as if ashamed, and Jack saw the tears running and looked away out of tact.

After a while he said gently, "Why?"

"Because my family has money?" She said it simply, without pride or shame but as a fact. "My husband loved me because I was a Rhode Island Brown."

Jack blinked. It was clear that didn't mean shit to him. "You die, he inherits."

She nodded vaguely and wiped her wet face with her good arm. "We hadn't been getting along for a while. And I had a paper in *Science* and one in *Nature* and he had a coauthor citation in *Aquatic Geochemistry*."

Jack studied her for a second, then took the pot to the creek and filled it for tea. At least they still had tea. Wynn knew the look and he knew what Jack was thinking: Poor Maia; damn. The lives that people twist themselves into. And also: Rich people are another species. Sort of lost in their own way. It's a good thing they have country clubs and shit because it keeps them kinda corralled up in one place. Jack had surely decided that neither one in that marriage of scientists was very appetizing.

Jack set the pot over the coals and let it boil for a few minutes and then he fetched the makings from the box and the two travel cups and brought them to the fire. They were very lucky that the box and bag had been strapped in so well and that the straps had held. They drank the sweet tea slowly, and when she was finished Jack took the cup from her and made his own. Wynn watched her and saw her head loll once as if she would pass out. He thought again that if she didn't get to a hospital soon she would die. Well, she was sitting against the stump and she was close enough to the heat—for now it was best to let her be. He sat away from the fire facing downstream where the woods were still green and standing and he worked the little chunk of wood in his hand with his knife. He heard a loon call, piercing and forlorn, and it poured into his spirit like cool water. It was a sad cry and he realized as he listened how barren the river had felt in the days without it. Why was a wail that seemed so lost and lonely so . . . what? Essential and lovely. It was like the blues, he guessed, or like Jack's cowboy songs. Sad, but somehow you would starve without them.

Wynn looked downstream at the course of sky curving away between walls of living woods. Soon the channel of firmament would pulse with a star, then three, then a hundred, and it would keep filling and deepening until the stars sifted and flowed between the tops of the trees in their own river, whose coves and bends would mirror the one they were on. He had thought it before, and he loved thinking about the two rivers. The river of stars would find its way to its own bay and its own ocean of constellations and Wynn imagined, as he had before, that the water and the stars might sing to each other in a key inaudible, usually, to the human ear. But probably you could hear it. Sometimes. If you quieted the pulse of your own blood. A rhythmic keening at the edge of sound. Wynn thought that if wolves sang, and coyotes, and elk and birds, and wind, and we, too, it was probably in response to a music we didn't know we could hear.

He thought about collecting embers from their fire and carrying them in the pot down to the river's edge and spreading them into a bending river. It would be beautiful once night fell. If he then blew on them they would breathe and shimmer with sparks. He could see it: the low throbbing light winding

through the dark. But it would not be quite like stars, and anyway the fire wasn't big enough and they didn't have enough
embers. She needed the heat.

No one realized how late in the afternoon it had gotten. The
sun dropped into the tall trees downstream and the air cooled
fast. Damn. They must have been sapped by hunger and
exhaustion, because they had let the afternoon slip away. Lost
it to lollygagging on the shore. No, they hadn't lost it: they had
badly needed the fish and the rest. Wynn thought how they
also needed to get downstream, to get her to a doctor if nothing else, and how it was unspoken but none of them wanted
to paddle into the blasts of a 12-gauge shotgun. Because that's
what was surely waiting. Wynn put the scaled-down canoe in
his pocket and went to the fire. She was stretched out—Jack
had fetched the foam pad—and she seemed to be asleep and
her bruised face was alarmingly pale.

Jack said, "Whoa. Big, you look like Frankenstein."

"Thanks."

"Hurt?"

"Not much."

Jack pushed off from the bench he'd made from rocks and
driftwood and went to the Pelican box and brought back a tube
of Neosporin. "Here, wash your hands off and use some of
this. Better if we let it breathe in open air than cover it. What
they told me when I burned my thigh on the Kawasaki."

"You did?"

"Fell over at like one mile an hour. A sizzling August afternoon. My inner thigh hit the motor and it made a sound I'd rather forget and smelled like pork chops."

"Gross."

"I jumped in the cow pond like a cartoon character. Bad idea. Not the cleanest water. By nightfall there were streaks running up my leg. Pop was at the Cattlemen's Association meeting in the Springs. I called my neighbor's mom, who was a nurse, and told her and she said, 'Jack, you listen to me. That's blood poisoning. It's serious shit. Things can fall off.' I looked down and saw how close it was to things and I drove myself straight to the ER."

Jack's hair was sticking out and he was immersed in the memory and wore a look of confounded horror. Wynn laughed. "You trying to scare me?"

"No, no. Sorry. You'll be fine. But we'll get it looked at as soon as we hit the village."

Wynn sat beside his buddy. "She doesn't look good."

"I was thinking that. Something's screwed up inside her. He hit her more than she told us about, or she blacked out."

"Should we try to make a couple of miles before full dark?"

Jack shook his head. "We won't get far. Plus we're safe here. If he'da been anywhere near we'd have known about it by now." Jack spat onto a chunk that had gone to ember and it hissed.

"We were really lucky up above. He missed us at forty feet with a shotgun. That won't happen again."

"You don't really like her."

Jack's head came around and he looked at Wynn and his eyes were dancing with the old mischief. "How should I know? Do you?"

Wynn shrugged. He pulled the canoe from his pocket and tugged free the clip knife and sprang it open with his thumb. He dug at the wood with the point where he was hollowing out the bow.

"You like her," Jack said. "She's your kinda gal. Smart, tough, no BS, probably pretty. She'd boss you around just like your mom."

"Hey!" Wynn grinned. It was good to have the old Jack back. "You don't like her?" he said. "I mean Maia. I know you love my bossy mom."

Jack snagged the tin of Skoal from his breast pocket, where it had miraculously stayed buttoned through the swim. It was still wet but chewable. He said, "I think she comes from a world I don't understand. That shit about competing publications. Why would you live like that?"

There was no answer forthcoming, but there was the contingent crackle of the fire and the wind fluttering through it. They were on the green side of the creek and they could hear loud crickets again. Jack said, "And how on God's earth could that lead to murder? Murdering your *wife*?"

"He must have been drunk."

"She didn't say that."

"No."

Jack said, "I've been thinking of that Windigo story you told me. The hungry ghost. And how the country has been drying up. And those people dying on the river last year. Like maybe the whole river is cursed. Like whatever stalked those folks in the village could turn a marital spat into murder."

Wynn remembered in a flash Jack pointing the gun above the last portage—his best friend. Had it been a real threat? He wasn't sure. He didn't say anything.

In the saying nothing and in the hushed tones of the fire there was a hum of something persistent and barely registered, the twang of a bass guitar string long seconds after the last note was struck. It thrummed the dusk almost without sound, like the quality of air before a lightning storm. Jack heard it first and sat up. Wynn stopped touching the edges of his burned face and listened.

It wasn't a lightning storm or music, it was a motor, distinct now, distant but growing closer, and it lacked the chuff and throb of an outboard, it was smoother, steadier, it thrummed through the twilight with the modest growl of an electric engine. It was the two drunks. Had to be. Jack and Wynn stood. They glanced at the woman asleep on the pad and trotted to the water. And stood there side by side like some backcountry couple who hear a strange car coming up the crick road for the first time in a year. Jack had a second thought and went back for the rifle. They waited in the dusk.

It was a gentle right bend and the long canoe appeared in the middle of it as if breached straight from the dark water, or as if the silvered water itself had formed and reformed until it gave substance to two shapes, the men, the two idiots, one thin, one fat, straining forward to interpret the flames they saw on the beach. The skinny one in the bow whistled, a piercing Bronx cheer that muted even the crickets for a startled second.

"Hey! Hey! Is it you-all?" That was the fat man.

Jack glanced at Wynn, who seemed stunned. Maybe by the dumbness of the greeting; maybe it was a trick question.

The fat man cursed. The canoe came ineluctably closer.

"Fuck a duck," the fat man said, very clear. "It's those kids. It's you kids!"

"The short one's got a gun," the thin one said.

"So what, everybody's got a gun up here. Hey! Hey! Fuckin' A, we're glad to see you-all!"

They came in like that, thrumming steadily over the dark mirror of the river, revealing the white square-tailed twenty-one-footer smirched with black, and one long gunwale, the starboard, edged and roughened with char where it had burned. "Fuckin' A! We thought you-all were crisp by now. *Damn!*"

There was something wrong with the electric motor, because it was louder than it should have been, it sounded almost like a blender, and the fat man drove the canoe straight into the rocky bar. The boat hit the stones and the two men jerked forward and back in practiced synchrony and the hull grated up onto the shore and the fat man throttled the motor two more times for good measure and cut the engine. He was grinning. He was wearing a camo Texas A&M cap and in the dusk he was all teeth. "Whew!" he said. "That was one hellstorm, wasn't it? We thought we were safe once it jumped, but a backdraft caught us. We shoulda waited a day. *Man.*" His eyes followed the creek. "Look at you-all. Just back into the green like any other Sunday. Hell, I woulda stopped here, too." He clambered forward, knees walking on the bags of gear, and got out on dry rocks and came at them with his hand out. The thin man hadn't budged—he was staring at the fire, at the person lying there, and Jack could almost hear the gears clicking in the man's head from ten feet away.

"Brent. Remember me?" Fat Man shook one boy's hand, then the other's. "I remember you! We shoulda listened. Man! We caught fire at sea like that destroyer, whatchamacallit?" The boys had no idea. "Almost punched our ticket, I mean. That was waaay too close for comfort. Glad you-all—" He stopped short. He looked into Wynn's face and grimaced. "Ow. You, too. That doesn't look too good," he said with real concern. "You boys came that close, too. I think we got some sterile bandages. JD—" He turned back to the boat and saw his buddy's face and followed his gaze. "Wha—?"

Brent peered into the dusk, glanced back at the boys. Jack unslung the rifle, which was not lost on anyone.

"There was just two of you before," Brent said softly.

Jack didn't say anything. Nor Wynn. They didn't know what to say. Neither had digested much of what they'd been through; what had happened since they'd met the men on their island was too immense.

The fat man worked his jaw, surveyed the little beach. "As far as I know there was only one other party up here—must've got dropped in at Moose Lake before us. A man and a woman in an Old Town. Green. A green eighteen-footer, I'd guess. We kept seeing them far off and wanted to stay out of their hair. We weren't in no hurry." The man spoke quietly but loud enough for his partner to hear. Jack watched as JD slowly slipped their Winchester bolt-action—probably an aught-six—out of its place under the bow deck: they had worked out the same configuration, pilot in the stern, shooter in the bow.

Brent was in no hurry now. He was a cool customer, for sure. He turned back again and looked each boy dead in the eye. It was as if he were searching for something inside them. Even in the half-light Jack could see, and remembered, the grainy mineral blue of the man's eyes.

"Looks like her. From here. Can't be sure. Same size, about. The long brown hair. Where's the man?"

Silence. The crickets were at it again, and the low burble of the current and the eddy slurping the shore. Wynn cleared his throat and opened his mouth and Jack touched him with the barrel of the rifle. Wynn's head swung around and he saw Jack's face and shut his mouth and swallowed.

"That's how it is, huh?" Brent said. "Some sort of *Deliverance* shit going on here and everyone's clammed up?" He chewed the corner of his mouth, frowned. "We got through the god-damned fire, and I mean that was nip and tuck. Thought we had clear sailing. Fuck." He turned his head sideways and spat. "You chewing?" he said to Jack. Jack nodded. "Give me a dip, will ya? I ran out in week two." Jack took his left hand off the rifle and unbuttoned the shirt pocket and handed the man the tin. "Thanks." Brent handed it back.

Jack said, "It's not what you think."

"No?"

"She's hurt bad. We're trying to get her out to a doctor. But—"

"I'm listening. With great interest, I surely am." Brent spat.

"Her husband did this. Threw our shit in the river at the first portage and paddled out."

Brent worked his jaw, cocked his ear sideways as if trying to hear the faint winds of logic.

"Then we flipped in that last big rapid, lost the rest of our food and warm clothes," Jack said.

It was getting darker. The tide of night seemed to flow up the river and settle over the water and spill over the banks. Ever so slowly. Where there were trees the gathering darkness was rising up into the shaggy tops, which had gone still. The sunset wind had nearly died. It was just a stirring of air upstream that came with a cool touch that presaged another night of frost.

For the first time in what seemed like years, Jack smelled less char than the cold scents of sediment-laden water.

He said, "It's a long story. We thought we were fucked. Now we need to get her out to the village. You can move a lot faster with that motor. Maybe you can take her at first light."

Brent studied Jack. And spat. Then he looked up at Wynn, who, even hunched, with his hands in his pockets, towered over them both. Even in the thickening dusk Wynn was all freckles and unruly curls and earnestness and seemed much more Norman Rockwell than James Dickey; he looked like a kid who had never had a mean thought in his life. Brent said, "You wanna put that rifle away somewhere?"

"If your man does."

Brent whistled softly and JD tucked the aught-six back under the bow. Jack slung the .308 over his shoulder. Brent said, "I owe you one, back at the island. We were on a little bit of a bender." His chuckle was mirthless. "Maybe we weren't paying attention to what we should have. The day after you left, JD climbed a tree. And we saw that motherfucking fire. We didn't get overcranked, but we kept an eye on it. So, thanks."

Jack nodded. "Okay, well," Brent said. "She's bad?"

Jack nodded again. Brent said, "We'll camp with you-all and take off at daybreak. Sound good? We've been fishing and we've got a bunch of extra food. Looks like you could use a good meal."

~

Jack and Wynn helped the men unload. They had a big wall tent, which skinny JD set up by himself with the light of a headlamp. He never said a word and he never got too far away from his gun. He seemed to be the muscle. Brent brought up only one dry bag, presumably with his own stuff, and went to the fire, where he tossed on a few sticks of driftwood and settled himself on a bigger rock. He looked over at the sleeping woman without expression. Wynn had covered her with his sleeping bag so only her head stuck out, and except for the fading bruises and the dark circles under her eyes, and what even in the moving firelight was an unnatural paleness, she looked like any other sleeping woman. Brent dug into his bag and brought out a full plastic fifth of Ancient Age and unscrewed the cap, drank. Jack watched him. Brent knew he was being watched and didn't seem to care. He had a second thought and roused himself and walked down in the dark to his boat and brought up a wire grill and what looked like a two-gallon plastic barrel with latches. With two sticks he shoved the blaze to one side of the fire ring and set up the grill on its legs over a heap of coals and unlatched the barrel and laid out four fat lake trout, evidently salted in brine. Yum. He nodded to himself at a job well done, sat back on the rock and busied himself with the serious business of drinking. When JD was done with the tent and unrolling the sleeping pads and carrying the kitchen box to the fire, he sat beside his buddy on the flat rock and took the fifth from Brent's hands without a word and took a long swallow. Jack figured he must have drunk three ounces in one go. Well. One way of making yourself at home.

The men were no fools. Nothing like Jack had thought on the first encounter on the lake. They made a big meal with wordless efficiency. Brent even deigned to peel potatoes they fished from a plastic burlap sack. Salted lake trout and potatoes and steamed carrots, and a bouillon gravy JD stirred up in a frying pan with flour and some nameless oil. Jack and Wynn let Maia sleep and set up the little tent so she could move into it later. As soon as she woke they'd feed her. The boys ate with ravenous hunger. Nobody said much. If JD and Jack kept track of where the rifles were at all times and kept them close, nobody let on that they noticed.

CHAPTER NINETEEN

The night was dark. The waning moon had come and gone, settling down like a curve of bone in a west where no smoke lingered. The stars and the flicker of northern lights on the eastern horizon had been doused in clouds. The campfire had nearly expired. Jack had let it die down. And he had let Wynn sleep. Wynn: laid out under the frost that never came, stretched out in the open under a night that smelled like rain, sleeping on the beach so he could let Maia have privacy in the tent. Wynn, who had said, "Cap, wake me in two hours. Let's do two-hour shifts tonight. No one's going to have any problem passing out." Jack had promised and sat by the fire with JD and watched the man drink. The two with their rifles lying beside them on the stones.

JD had offered, proffered the now half-full bottle of bourbon by the neck, and Jack had taken the bottle the first two times. He knew with drinkers that the first impression was the thing, that once you started knocking back with a serious drinker they'd just assume you were with them all night, matching them slug for slug, even if you never took another sip. To a drinker, everyone else in the world was a partyer, too. So he got JD launched, which wasn't hard because the two fishermen had probably been drinking all day. Jack wouldn't have been surprised if one of the boxes in the canoe was solid fifths.

Brent had hit the hay early, muttering, "Big day tomorrow," and keeping whatever thoughts to himself. JD drank with a steady sullenness. Between bouts, he swung his head and watched Jack from under his brow, and if he wanted to ask what the hell had happened with the girl, et cetera, he restrained himself, but he turned his head to the tent more than once and Jack had the strong impression that it wasn't just because he had burning questions. There was a young woman lying in there, however injured. That's the sense Jack got.

Jack watched him like a wolf. He was smelling the man as much as watching him. Smelling him getting more stewed, watching for signs of fatigue. He needed these guys, and he wasn't going to screw it up. A light wind came up, moving downstream, and it chilled his back. Good. An owl hooted. Single hollow notes whose cadence Jack followed to keep himself awake. But they never formed a pattern, except that in their staggered randomness they seemed to probe a night of velvet depths and echoing solitude. He stirred up the fire and added wood to keep the heat coming, more to lull JD than to warm himself. He needed to stay awake.

And he did, barely.

~

There's a certain stillness before dawn. A caesura. The fire was a heap of dusted embers. No wind. In the lacuna between out-breath and inbreath even the owl hushed. The sipping of the river seemed to drop an octave. *Fuck.* Jack's head jerked up. He must have passed out. Even he couldn't vanquish the exhaustion of the past couple of days. He must have slept sitting up, slumped over the rifle in his lap, and now he stirred and his head twitched up, and he shook it and straightened his back against the stiffness. *Fuck.* He sucked in a draft of cold air. Something had woken him. Wha—?

He heard an animal. Tussling, squeaking near the woods. He swung around. It wasn't the woods, it was . . . what? There was Wynn, stretched flat on his back, dead to the world on the stones. It was no animal. He heard squeaking and a muffled cry and looked farther in the half dark and saw the man JD's boots sticking out of the unzipped door of the tent.

~

He moved. If he had ever moved that fast—he scooped up the rifle and was at the tent in twelve strides. The man's gun was lying on the rocks. He kicked it away over the stones. And then in one movement Jack shifted the grip on his rifle and slammed the butt into the man's kidneys. An explosive grunt. In the next second he was dragging him out by his belt with one hand, and when his head was clear of the flap he heard him utter, "Not! Not what you think!" and Jack dropped him like a bale of hay and with both hands he swung the stock of the Savage 99 hard across the side of the man's head. An awful thwack and the man slumped to the stones.

He heard crying and reached back into the tent and whispered fast, "It's okay, it's okay, it's Jack. We're leaving now, getting away." He put his hands in and half pulled, half urged her out.

She was awake, thank God. She was swimming up out of some nightmare. Her eyes unblurred and he could see that she was replaying the last minutes like a film, he could see her mind spinning fast. She gripped his arm in the near dark and nodded. She stood. Shaky. He reached past her and pulled out the pad and sleeping bag and crumpled them in his left arm.

"We're going, we're going, we're leaving," Jack whispered, harsh. "Can you walk?"

She nodded. She was breathing hard, maybe hyperventilating. "Okay," he said. He took her elbow with his right hand and guided her fast, as fast as they could, down toward Wynn and the shore. When they got to the sleeper, Jack released her and crouched, shook Wynn hard, moved the cap off his face where it lay and shook, and when Wynn uttered *"Hey,"* half in sleep, he put his hand over his mouth.

Wynn groaned and his eyes sprang open and Jack's fingers went to his lips. Wynn blinked twice, then nodded in his bag. Jack made a downward pressing gesture with his open hand— *Keep it superquiet.*

Wynn roused himself and picked up his pad and sleeping bag and followed, confused. The three of them were now in the dark like ghostly revenants of the river upstream, the upstream side of the creek where everything was burned and the trees were bone. Because they moved without sound and were lit only by starlight, and were so depleted and rattled by the past days that they walked to the water's edge in a hitching trance. Two did. Jack urged them on. They headed for the boats. Jack held Maia's arm and kept looking back at the dull glow of coals that was the remains of the fire and at the shadow of the wall tent. They moved toward the boats and then Wynn drifted right, down toward their canoe, and Jack whistled without sound, just a hushed blow, and jerked his head, kept moving toward the Texans' square-tail beached twenty feet upstream. Maia hesitated. Jack tugged her elbow and she followed. They tiptoed as best they could over the stones. Jack felt for the slung rifle on his back and piled in the sleeping gear and went swiftly to the bow and lifted and began to push and slide the men's canoe. Very slowly, easing the hull so it barely scraped. Maia stopped. She swayed on the beach and lifted her hands. A questioning gesture, even in the dark. Jack pointed to the stern, which was in the water, pointed, emphatic: *Get in.* Put his finger to his lips again. He got the boat nearly free of shore and then Wynn said, full-voiced, "Hey, hey, Jack. What the fuck? Why're you taking their boat?"

He was standing almost to the water halfway between the two canoes, holding his bundled sleeping bag and pad. "Let's take ours." He was backlit by a sheen of river suffused with starlight.

"Jesus, Wynn!" Jack hissed, just above a whisper. "C'mon! Shut up and get over here!" He looked back past the fire. The dark shape of JD, crumpled on the rocks, was moving, straightening. Fuck. "Maia, jump on. Now! In the center."

She did. Somehow. More a fall than a jump, but she was in. Jack shoved. The hull of the men's canoe grated loudly. The bow cleared rock and floated free. "Wynn, get in! *Now!*" He was no longer whispering. He was walking his hands quickly down the port gunwale to the stern, wading heedlessly hip-deep into the river and he vaulted into the stern. He heard a clatter of stone and saw JD standing, getting his bearings, heard the curses. Jack found the push start on the grip of the motor and pressed it. He'd grown up trolling with these suckers. It clicked and whirred and started, thank God. He thumbed the reverse lever and twisted the throttle as the canoe was being swept upshore with the eddy current, revved the prop and backed the boat to where Wynn was standing like a fucking tree, his arm spread out in protest. Jack glanced up the shore past the embered fire and saw JD swaying, looking for his gun. He was probably trying to clear his head. Oh man. "Wynn!" Jack shouted now and the night echoed it back like the owl's sad hoot. "He tried to *rape* her! Get the fuck in! *Now!Now!Now!Now!*" and out of the corner of his eye he caught the movement. In just a couple of minutes the air must have grayed just enough, gathered the grains of light enough, because he saw the man, the fat man, bolt from the big tent, moving fast, surprisingly fast, not to them but to their little tent and JD, his one shout, *"Sonofabitch!"* a cry of protest at every cross-grained turn of events, and he shoved JD sprawling again to the rocks and swept up the rifle. Maybe Wynn saw him too because he lurched out of his paralysis—he leapt toward the water and the rifle cracked, a single sharp note, and Wynn spun and flew backward into the river.

If Jack shouted nobody heard, the shot reverberated and deafened. He revved the throttle, the boat jumped back, and he let go the motor and somehow leaned and doubled to water with both hands and hauled in his buddy by shirt and shoulders, dragged and dumped him over the lip of the gunwale, hot blood running over his cold hands, and more shots split the air and thudded into the hull. He flipped the lever forward and twisted and the canoe lurched and then he was gunning for the top of the eddy and the guard rock there and angling hard into the passing current, aiming for the tightest line around the bend. Upriver. He was going upstream, not down. Wynn was gasping and moaning, eyes rolling, and the woman screamed and the motor blared. The man must have been emptying the magazine because another shot split the air and another shattered off the back of the engine cover and stung Jack's hand. Fat Man could surely shoot in the near dark. As they rounded the bend and out of range they heard the primal roar, something between a demon's growl and an animal scream, and one more shot, and Jack thought that maybe Brent had just blasted JD on the spot for sheer frustration and he hoped he hadn't. He knew he hadn't. Because Brent was essentially a decent man who had just shot a decent kid. Because Jack had stolen their boat.

CHAPTER TWENTY

Wynn died as the sun broke over the trees. A clear morning, no fog and cloudless. He died staring up at the new sun while Jack tried to stanch the blood that welled out of his chest with every heartbeat. First with his bare hands, then with his two shirts, then with his own body, hugging Wynn tight as he died. Jack had gunned the heavy boat a quarter mile upstream and across the river and tied it to a scorched root and flung himself at Wynn, who by then was whimpering less, just gasping, bubbling, and staring up into his friend's face and then past him to the sun, and Jack covered him and hugged him to his own chest and he died.

Jack howled. Howled into his own muffling arms—the scream that was not for Brent to hear. To the men downriver they had to be long gone.

CHAPTER TWENTY-ONE

Jack could see it in his mind's eye: the rage. Breaking camp in silent fury. Loading the much smaller canoe with the cook box, the barrel of brined fish, the massive tent roll. No whiskey. Plenty of space in the nineteen-footer without the case of Ancient Age. Not a single bottle left. Maybe the most ire-inducing fact of all.

Reloading the rifle. Thumbing the cartridges in the magazine one by one, each with a curse and a prayer for more death. *We helped them. We gave aid and succor to those sonsofbitches and look at what they did. Goddamn. Probably keeping the girl drugged or some such, some slave. Well, I plugged one, surely did, hope he's dead. But why in hell did they go* upstream?

The useless sentry, JD. Brent backhanding him maybe, full force across the already bruised jaw. Muttering maybe about how a professional drinker who can't hold his liquor or holster his hard-on is the saddest thing on earth. Loading the pinewood-colored Kevlar canoe, shoving off, hellbent for

Wapahk. Three days hence. Paddling with a will, because a) no bourbon, b) no food but a few salted fish, c) vengeance. The phone there in the village, the urgent call to the Mounties: *Send a chopper. One injured or drugged girl, two bad men, one injured or dead.* Because Brent was sure that the same laws held on a northern river as they did in Texas: if you caught someone stealing your horse you could shoot him dead, no questions asked.

Jack could imagine the two Texans paddling hard in his and Wynn's canoe and reaching the rock island in the bend before the infamous Last Chance Falls, heading toward shore. And . . .

And the man Pierre waiting, loaded, for two men in their Kevlar nineteen-footer. Waiting head down behind his cover, and . . . there it was, the canoe, correct length and color—the boys! Sitting ducks, no gun in sight! His blurred, uncorrected vision plenty good enough at forty yards to see two male figures steadily paddling. Patience, brother, waiting until they were maybe thirty, twenty-five yards off the shore, rising up, shotgun leveled—*fire!* Pump, *fire,* pump, *fire* . . . until he had emptied the six shells in the Winchester Marine, the men torn open and flung sidelong, the canoe flipped, a bobbing loglike hull in the main current, tugged toward the horizon line, tipping over the lip of the cataract. Gone.

Smashed and drowned.

Pierre would think that if she was still with them he wouldn't have to worry about her either. She would have been lying half alive in the bottom of the boat, she would be battered to death and submerged in the terrible falls.

The odds of finding bodies in this big river, in this remote territory, were pretty low. But if they did, if the authorities mounted
an ambitious search and there were gunshot wounds, he could
say that the boys had attacked their camp, kidnapped her, he
ambushed them, it was survival, self-defense, he was trying to
rescue her.

Jack replayed how Pierre would shoot the two men from Texas
thinking they were he and Wynn, and then Pierre would pack
up his camp, relieved that it was finally over, his megafuckup,
and he would go straight to the village elders and start spout-
ing lies.

Jack's plan. Why he had stolen their boat. Why Wynn was
dead. Everybody he loved most, he killed. One way or another.
Hubris killed them—his own. Always.

~

Still, he'd have to wait a day to let it play out. Wait upstream
with a woman who was clearly dying, and with the body of his
best friend.

CHAPTER TWENTY-TWO

He didn't wait a day. She was dying and he couldn't just sit. At what he figured was noon he shoved off.

Jack paddled. He saved the motor, the battery, for the upstream wind he knew would come. He paddled the green woods, the woods with birds. With a fat kingfisher flying off a limb, lilting along river's edge, perch to living perch. A lone osprey. He watched the woman, curled into the thwart, maybe sleeping, too pale, breath shallow—he watched the back of her raingear for the slight lift of an inhalation and sometimes he couldn't see it and he said aloud, *"Please, please breathe. Breathe . . ."* He paddled harder than he ever had in his life. He did not look at his friend's curls ruffling in the wind, the almost ginger curls alive in the breeze as on any day, Wynn's head, Wynn's cheek on his arm where Jack had laid him in the front of the boat as if sleeping.

If he saw the woods, the gravel bars, the steep banks sailing by . . . he paddled. His hands and arms went numb. His mind, too. His thoughts untethered and it was as if he were paddling blind.

~

On the day of his mother's service Jack woke at first light and in the fog of waking remembered why he had to get away. He dressed and hurried out of the log house. A June morning with a mist lying in the tall grass of hayfields that waited for the first cutting. He could smell the sweetness in the grass. Above a low ridge scattered with junipers he could see north and east the snow ramparts of the Never Summer range floating in the wash of the first sun. He turned. The barn across the yard was decorated with bunches of pine boughs and cattails, bouquets of dried wildflowers nailed to the frame around the big door. Many neighbors had come by the day before and brought handmade wreaths of spruce and fir, armloads of every flower that now bloomed and could be gathered.

He could not look at them. He went through the barn. The swept concrete, the empty stalls, the smell of horses. Mindy, his mother's mare, was not there. He went through and out the back and climbed the rail fence into the pasture. The horses were scattered, heads down. In the mist it looked almost like they were feeding in pale water.

She was down at the bottom of the field where the pasture dropped off into the willows on the banks of the Fraser. The heavily dewed grass wet his pant legs to the knees. As he got closer he could hear the big-boned quarterhorse tearing at the bunched grass, hear her huff, and then he could smell her. She was the color of a saddle wet with rain.

He walked to her and she lifted her head and turned. He said, "Hey, girl. Hey." He put a hand on her neck and she pushed into the side of his cheek with her nose and her hot breath puffed into the collar of his shirt. Her right foreleg was wrapped with bandage. When she stepped to him she lurched as if hobbled. He leaned his forehead into her at the base of her neck and she stayed still. He let his hand travel lightly over her rippled ribs, which the vet said had been broken. She did not flinch. She was his mother's favorite horse. She let the boy lean into her.

Jack stood with her. He didn't make a sound. He leaned into her and inhaled. Here was the last place his mother had been. Before the crashing water. Been at peace. Humming along with his father, who sang. He thought that. You were here. Now you're not. He would have given his own life gladly to hear her sing to him one more time. He put his face hard into the mare's side and let himself go. He wrapped his arms around the mare's neck as best he could. He didn't move.

After a while Mindy turned suddenly and lurched into him and he saw his father coming over the sunlit pasture.

He was wearing a sport coat and he didn't say anything. He didn't say, "I've been looking for you." He came up to the boy and the mare and he put one hand on his son's head and one on the flank of the horse and just stood. Stood for a while. Jack wished they could stay like that. Finally his father said, "It's time."

They walked back to the barn. His father kept his hand on him, his shoulder, his head. Many people spoke. Someone played a song on a guitar. They spoke again. People wept. Some laughed through tears. He couldn't make out the words. He stood in the deep shadow of a makeshift platform. Then he felt his father touch him and he heard him say, "Jack? Jack, can you say a word? Just something. Anything?" He felt himself nod. He stepped up onto the platform. All he could see was sunlight. He said . . . nothing. He froze. That was it. The air was full of sun. Nobody spoke. What could he say when this was all his fault? His mouth moved and no sound came out and he began to spin. And then he heard a rush like wind and the thump of his father's boots on the planks and his father's big hand on his shoulder and heard, "Jack. It's okay, son, that's okay," and he felt his father lift him. He lifted him skyward and covered him. He covered him and squeezed him tight and held him, all the time whispering, "Let's get something to eat. It's okay, it's okay . . ."

Jack didn't snap out of it until he heard a rush like surf. He woke up and he was paddling hard and his tears were falling into the skim of water in the bottom of the canoe, the water that was pink with Wynn's blood. No wind, the air very still; they must not have needed the motor. The evening had chilled and the sun was in the tops of the trees on the left shore. And then he was fully awake as from a dream and he started with panic because he knew the rush was the falls and he knew they needed to get to the left bank. He sucked in a deep long breath, *fuck,* and he found her with his eyes and what of her face he could see was white, too white, but he saw the slight lift of her breathing and blew out in relief. He did not look at Wynn's head lying there on his arm in the bow, he looked past it and felt the pull of the swift current downstream toward the flat horizon line and roar, the lip of the falls, and gauged the distance to the open stretch of cobbled beach he could see, which must be the take-out and the portage, and the thought flashed: *We might not make it.* He dropped the paddle against the seat and reached back and toggled the switch and pushed the starter and the engine chafed and hummed to life, thank God. He shoved the throttle arm hard away and pushed the boat into a steep left arc and swung the bow up into the current at a ferry angle toward the left bank. And then he stood in the stern and scanned. With his free hand he shucked the .308 from where he'd stuck it into the strap of a food-box, barrel down. He tugged it free and gunned the engine full throttle and was surprised again at the power of the electric motor, good, and he sat and held the tiller with his knee and shouldered up the rifle and scanned.

He kept both eyes open and looked through the scope. He let the crosshairs travel over the bank and back and then farther into the tall grass and fireweed and then back into the big pines that stood at the edge of the woods. Nothing. If everything had gone down the way he thought it had, then Pierre would be long gone, probably in the last miles approaching Wapahk, where he would begin weaving lies as fast as he could talk.

Good. But. Still. He scanned, and he could see with relief that he had ferried far enough to make the beach, and he throttled back and slowed and stood and he scanned the beach and the trees with his naked eye and then took up the rifle again and covered every rock and tree and shadow with the scope. Nothing. Good. He did not relax. He was not going to fuck up now.

He slung the rifle and gunned the heavy canoe onto the stones of the shore, heedless of gouges, and he hopped out fast where the stern was still in the water and he splashed the shallows almost at a run until he had gotten around to the front and he grabbed the bow and heaved back hard so the canoe was high on dry rocks and then he ran. He unslung the .308 from his shoulder and ran up the beach and dove into the fireweed and circled back down. He moved with the lightness and speed of a hunt when the bull elk had lifted his nose in alarm and bolted from the meadow. He was not going to get shot now. Not now. He slowed and came down through big scattered pines, eyes following the startled flight of a flycatcher, a shift in the shadow of a limb, the lift of a moth. Nothing. And then he saw it. The glint of stainless steel in tall grass. In the long light that cut through the pines. Stainless steel, and two careful steps and he saw the shining length of the barrel, the wooden forestock of the 12-gauge, and then the man's arm. Outflung. In a green plaid shirt. The arm, the torso twisted back as if arched, the dark curls of the head and a black fleece hat a foot away in the grass. And the wool shirt caked in dried blood and one neat bullet hole in the center of the breast.

~

Pierre, you fucker. Good riddance.

He didn't feel a thing.

He crouched fast, and now he moved as low as he could to the ground, tree to tree, stopping often to listen. He knew Brent and JD would be long gone, but he'd also known that Pierre would have shot the Texans and he'd been wrong. He wasn't going to get plugged by Brent now. He moved tree to tree as the shadows of the pines lengthened over the beach and broomed over the stones. He covered the shore and then plunged down the easy trail around the falls and— Nothing.

He ran back to the top and cast around in the brush for Pierre's canoe—he thought if he could find the sat phone he could call in a chopper—but there was no canoe. Damn. Where had he stashed it? Wherever it was, he'd done a good job. Jack looked for sign, for drag marks, and saw nothing. Fuck it. He didn't have time to screw around any longer. Anyway, Pierre had probably tossed the phone in the river so the authorities wouldn't find it when he got to the village and ask why he hadn't called in an emergency earlier.

Jack went to the boat and lifted her and carried her as gently as he could around the roar of crashing whitewater to the launch beach below and laid her carefully on a thick bed of lichen and moss and ran back up and made himself carry Wynn. Wynn was much too heavy. He was unwieldy with the stiffness, but Jack got under him and heaved himself standing, and he kept him on his shoulder all the way down the trail, and though his knees buckled twice he did not let him drop. His ear and chin were against the cold skin of Wynn's right side above his belt, and he made himself talk the whole way: "Okay, buddy, we've got this, we've got this, we're going home now. I'm taking you home." Over and over. And then he ran back to the top beach and did not look again at Pierre sprawled in the shadows, and he slid the canoe up onto the wheely thing and took almost none of the provisions or gear, they just had to get through the night, and he bumped and heaved the lightened boat down the trail of the portage, and he laid her back into the boat on a bed of empty dry bags and murmured, *"Please please please,"* and he laid Wynn as best he could over the front seat, and then he shoved off and did not look back at the falls. He knew it was only forty-three swift-water miles to the village. Three days on a normal trip, but he knew they could navigate it safely at night and that they'd be there sometime tomorrow.

EPILOGUE

Jack drove.

The steep twisting road up Dusty Ridge. He drove with his lights off, because it was not yet full night and he wanted to see all the woods and the sandy track going through them. He hit holes filled with the afternoon's rain that splashed up onto the hood of the truck, and when the wind blew, it gusted water and leaves out of the trees and spattered his windshield.

Though it was a cold October night he drove with the windows down and he could hear Sawyer Brook rushing in its banks. He knew every turn and every big maple. He had driven the road who knew how many times. He had driven it mostly with Wynn, and driven it alone when Wynn was studying for some exam and he had already finished and was hankering for family to come home to. It was not his home, but it was close—they had made him feel so. He loved almost more than anything the singsong call of Wynn's mother, Hansie, as he came through the door: "Jack? Jaaack? Is it you? Come in, come in! Wynn called, said you'd be here. How wonderful, come in!" That song. And the smells would hit him, of a family in the midst of their lives, the morning's bread on the board, the woodstove, stone scent of the slate at the entrance crumbed with mud, the Lab, Leo, knocking the leg of a table with his tail, the pine and oak exhalations of the old house. The smells wafted in intertwining tendrils and filled a space in him he was used to having empty. It was almost painful.

Tonight he drove the twisting dirt road with dread. He had not come to the funeral. It had been in late September, three weeks after the trip had ended. It was maybe Wynn's favorite time of year to be on the ridge. The woods yellow and flushed to almost the color of honey, and you could smell the apples ripening on the trees down the hill. And they had held the service in one of his favorite spots, the old hayfield that ran to Sawyer Brook where his mother, mostly, had taught him to fish. They had graciously asked Jack to come, and to say something. He was already at home on the ranch, and he had said, "I'm sorry, I can't."

"You can't?" Hansie said. That hadn't occurred to her.

"I just can't."

There was a pause—it sounded like wind through the line—and Hansie had said, "I don't blame you. Who would? Nobody does."

"Well."

"You blame yourself, it's crazy. I mean it, Jack. *God*. Just come. Please come. You know he'd want nothing more than that."

Electronic wind.

He could hear her huff. She said, "He told me once that he didn't even know where you came from."

"He did?"

"He said you were the best friend he'd ever had, it was like God or someone dropped you out of the sky onto that trail, and he never hoped to have another one so good. Like a brother but better, because you didn't have to grow up fighting. *God.*"

Well. He could hear Wynn saying that. Not wanting to leave God out of it and maybe hurt His feelings in case He really was up there *ex machina*-ing all over the place. He thanked her and told her he had to go help his father now. That was all he could manage. He wondered for the first time in his life if he was a coward.

But two weeks later he climbed into his truck and drove east. They had not registered for the fall quarter and he had no idea what he was going to do or even if he was going to return to school in the winter. He asked his dad if it was okay if he was back in May and he drove east. He drove across the high desert and the Great Plains, he drove all night. He tried to make himself not think of anything. It was already late in the day when he got to Putney.

The forests at the edge of the fields were luminous with yellows and pinks. The waning light could not mute them. He had already lived one autumn and he was having to live it again. He had no cell signal for some reason and he pulled into the grocery store of the Putney Co-op and asked to use the phone.

"Hello?" Hansie asked, uncertain. She sounded ragged.

"It's Jack."

"Oh." Indrawn breath.

"I'm in town. At the co-op. I was wondering if I could come up."

A freighted silence, carrying who knew what.

Finally: "You're here? In Putney?"

"Yes."

"Now?"

"Yes."

A rustling.

"George is away. He's designing a school in Craftsbury."

"I'm sorry." He didn't know why he said that. "I can come back another time."

"*No*. No, no, no. Come up. For God's sake. You can stay in Wynn's room."

No, I can't, he thought. I have my sleeping bag.

He bought two bottles of good red wine, he didn't even know what kind, the price card said thirty-two dollars, and he got back in the truck and drove up the hill west out of town. He passed the sturdy painted clapboard houses and the elementary school and turned up West Hill and the houses became sparser. The road climbed steeply. At a green sign that said Brelsford Road he took the left and drove up to the house that sat above the field.

He held the two wine bottles by the neck in his left hand. When she opened the door he didn't know what to do with his right hand. He held it out, expecting a handshake or nothing, and she came against it and put her arms around his shoulders and squeezed, squeezed hard, and let her head rest against him. Her hair smelled like woodsmoke and he could see the few rough strands of white. It occurred to him then that he was the last person to see her son alive, that if she was hugging him, she was also hugging Wynn. Goosebumps ran down his arms and he brought his free hand to her back and he held her. He could feel her ribs and she felt frail. It was the first time he'd thought that. He expected his shirt to be wet when she pulled away but it wasn't.

"It's good to see you," she said, not looking at him, and took the bottles. She looked disheveled. Her hair, often in a long braid, was loose. He walked in. He could smell a roast. Jess was at the table, drawing on a sketch pad, her tongue in the corner of her mouth. She looked up and seemed startled. She opened her mouth and her eyes lit and then he could see the confusion. That this time was not like the others.

"Hi," he said. "Hi, Jess."

"Hi." She closed the sketchbook. He didn't ask her what she was drawing.

"Where's Leo?" he said.

"Dad took him."

"Oh. Oh, good."

She moved her lips around and blinked fast and he could see the fingers of her good hand bending the corners of the sketch paper. "He likes road trips," she said.

"Oh, good. Yeah, I remember." He said, "I was thinking of running up the mountain early in the morning. Do you wanna come?"

She shook her head. "No, that's all right." She wouldn't look at him.

Hansie took a deep breath. "Take your jacket off and sit," she said. "We're ready."

He did. She opened one of the wine bottles. She used an old-style simple corkscrew and he noticed that she paused, almost as if to summon her concentration, before she screwed it into the cork swiftly and true and rocked the cork out with two motions. She forked the roast from the oven pan onto a platter and set it on the table.

"It's from Littledale, down the hill. We bought half a steer this year."

He nodded. "Smells good," he said. "His cows were always way better than ours."

They ate. He faced the big window, out of which, in daylight, he knew he could look down the folded hills and orchards to the Connecticut River Valley and across to Mount Monadnock. They ate in silence. Hansie put down her fork and took a long sip of wine. She left only enough to color the top of the stem of the glass. She turned to Jack.

"It was a beautiful service. He would've—" She stopped herself.

He didn't know what to say.

"What have you been doing?" she said. The edges of her eyelids were raw.

He didn't know how to answer. He might have said, *Combing over every hour of the month of August, then parsing them into minutes.* "Helping Pop gather," he said.

"The cows? Like a roundup?"

"Yes, off the mountain. The Never Summers."

"You're on horseback, right? I remember. Like a cowboy song, Wynn said." He saw her freckled hand reach blindly for the stem of her empty glass. He picked up the bottle and poured the glass full.

"Yes, ma'am," he said. She blinked. He'd never called her that, not since their first meeting, when, laughing, she had given him endless shit. She started to say something but didn't. Jack thought she was having trouble getting a full breath, and he looked away. He looked down at the table. Wynn had made the table for his parents' wedding anniversary—clear cherry. The tree must heve been very old, the grain was dark and tight. The grain of the wood was like the contours of a topographic map and he would have given a lot to walk into a country with that much wildness and rhythm and relief. Across the table she was trying to be silent, and he looked up only when she wiped her eyes with her napkin.

"You came a long way," she said.

He went stock-still. He didn't breathe.

"You need to tell it, and I need to hear it. Jess, too. She can hear it," she said.

"Hear it?"

"Jack."

He felt a surge of panic, maybe like a calf when it feels the first bite of the rope before branding.

"You want me to tell how we . . . ? All of it?"

Hansie nodded.

"Jess?" he said. The girl's eyes were wide and shiny. He saw that the slice of meat on her plate was uneaten. Her mother in her distraction had forgotten to cut it up. "Hey," he said. "Hey,

Jess, I'm sorry. You want me to cut it up for you?" She nodded without taking her eyes off him, and he reached across with his knife and fork and cut the beef into pieces.

He heard a tree branch ticking one of the windows. He owed them.

"Well," he said. "I—" He set his knife and fork on the plate. "Sure," he said. He wiped his mouth with his napkin and laid it on the table beside his plate, he didn't know why. As if at the end of the telling he would get up and go. He might.

"It began with us smelling smoke," he said. He glanced at Hansie.

She nodded.

"Okay. Well. We climbed a hill on an island and saw the fire. It was so big. It scared us. And then a morning with a heavy frost and a thick fog and a lot of wind."

He told it. The fog, the voices, how it was Wynn who insisted that they paddle back and tell the couple about the fire. Wynn was always taking care of people. He told about the man coming around the bend alone, about finding the woman. They watched his face. Jess's eyes were wide, almost as if she were watching a thriller she couldn't tear away from, and she kept twisting her napkin. The only sound was the knocking of the branch and an occasional gust buffeting the windows, whistling in the stove pipe. Now and then their drawn breaths. They didn't want him to slow down or stop.

He told about the woman's injuries, the near ambush, the fire. How they walked back into the burn. He didn't tell about the calf or the bear and her cub on the beach. When he got to meeting the Texans again and the night and the man in the tent and them hurrying down the beach toward the two canoes in the dark, he stopped himself. He turned his chair away, toward the stove. He just breathed. They hadn't shed a single tear since the beginning and he owed them.

"Okay," he said. Turned back.

"I took their canoe because it had a motor," he said. "She needed to get out as fast as we could get her and there was no way I was sending her with them." He reached for the Skoal in his shirt pocket without thought, untwisted the lid, put in a dip. "Also, after what happened I didn't want them to catch up with us."

"Here." Hansie slid him her teacup from the afternoon. It was rude to chew at dinner—what was wrong with him?

"I'm okay," he said, and swallowed.

She watched him closely. He coughed into his fist. "And because I wanted to protect my best friend and this woman. At all costs."

Her eyes bored into him. He said, "That's why I went upstream. I wanted the Texans to lead. I knew he—the man Pierre— would be waiting with his gun." He made himself look at her. She nodded. He was not looking for a reprieve and she did not give him one; it was as if she barely saw him. If she were anywhere, she was on that beach.

He told them how the fat man had shot Wynn. He told them that Wynn had died instantly. It was the only lie he told. He told about motoring down to Wapahk. He had given the Texans half a day and then paddled and motored all day and night. He told how he'd come to the portage at Last Chance and found Pierre. The shock. How he carried first the woman, then Wynn around the falls. How two Cree boys were on the dock when they got to the village at daybreak, and when they saw him they ran up the road. The Texans had come in the night before in a sleek expedition canoe raving about men being shot, a woman kidnapped. The men said they had come around the corner at Last Chance and angled toward the left shore and when they were twenty yards from the take-out beach this crazy sonofabitch had popped out from behind a tree and shot at them. With a 12-gauge. But he was clearly not a shooter and he didn't seat the stock and he blasted high. The fat one had told it and he said his partner JD might have been hungover and he might be a fuckup, but he was a good and loyal friend and he had been a Marine—that's where he and Brent had met—and he plugged the man Pierre in the chest as easily as he would shoot a deer startled in a clearing. He shot him just as Pierre let off another wild blast that this time shredded the limbs of the pine as he fell.

The village had called up to Churchill and Churchill had sent a Mountie named Austin McPhee. McPhee had married a Cree girl from Wapahk and so he was family and the town was relieved. He flew in on an Otter that night and had already interviewed the Texans and had asked them to be patient and had kept them under guard at the rec center. So Mountie McPhee was already there when the kids ran into town yelling about a wild man with a scoped Savage slung on his back and the wounded girl in the canoe with Wynn.

Hansie and Jess would not take their eyes off Jack. It was as if his face would give some lie to the telling, that he would crack and say, "No, not really. None of this happened. Wynn will be home tomorrow." Instead he said, "We carried her up to town on a stretcher behind a four-wheeler and they called back the Otter. We took her and Wynn to the airstrip in two separate trucks. McPhee flew back with them to the health center and returned the next morning with two more Mounties. They kept me in the back of the rec center away from the men and interviewed everyone separately. I guess they were afraid I would try to kill them. But I hadn't shot anyone, and the Texans weren't pressing charges about the boat. So they said they'd take me back to Churchill on the next flight and arrange another plane back to Pickle Lake, where we—I—had my truck." Was he telling them what they needed to know? He wasn't sure.

He said, "They said you-all had already arranged about getting Wynn home." Why hadn't he called them then?

"We did," Hansie murmured. "Then what?"

"Does it matter?"

"Yes."

"Okay." Somehow in the telling he had drunk his wine. He reached for the bottle, poured half a glass carefully, drank it down. He said, "McPhee said, given all the circumstances,

the Crown or whatever did not foresee charging the Texans.
There's, uh—" He held himself tight. Why now? He'd gotten
through the hardest parts.

He said, "The Mountie said preventing a man from stealing
your boat in the wilderness can be considered self-defense."
He took a breath. "Well, and—considering the confusion, heat
of the moment . . ."

She had squeezed her own napkin into a ball. Now she looked
at it in her palm like a crumpled dove and laid it out on the
table and smoothed it, folded it. She said, "What about the
rape? The attempt?"

"The man JD said he was just checking on her since he was
the only one awake. She couldn't tell which man it was in the
dark, and though she knew he was trying to molest her, in her
half-conscious state she wasn't sure of much more than that."

Hansie blew out. She refused to cry again. He wished she
would. Jess was looking from her mother to Jack, covering her
curled right hand with her good one as if she were trying to
protect it from the story.

Jack said, "They held the Texans, I guess, in Thunder Bay for
two days. That was it. The woman Maia had a perforated intes-
tine, broken ribs. McPhee told me that they said she would
fully recover."

Hansie said, "She called us. She was at Brigham and Women's.
We talked for an hour."

Jack looked up sharply. Of course she did. He was the only one who hadn't. Hadn't come across. Because in his heart he was still on the river. Right then he realized that was why. He was still on the river with Wynn and they were still paddling and they were still arguing about how much slack they should give the man, everyone. They were still fishing a tea-colored creek with watergrass in the bottom, wading up the stream, separated by a few yards. Wynn was making sculptures of rock and feathers on the shore. Thingamajigs. And reading to him from a book of ghost stories by the fire. This was Wynn's mother and sister, they were trying to move on. He wasn't.

"Gimme a minute," he said. "Please." He stood. He went out into the windy dark that smelled sweet of decaying leaves and stood on the little deck and packed his pipe and lit it. In a minute he would go back in. He would tell them whatever else they wanted to know.

But he wouldn't tell them how a Cree deputy had met him at the airport in Churchill and driven him to the Aurora Hotel. How he hadn't gone in. That he'd turned around and walked up Bernier Street past the ramshackle houses and rusted Ski-Doos and down to the shore. The tide was out, and he walked past the wreck of an outboard motorboat half buried in the sand and he walked straight out onto the tidal flat. He'd seen the polar bear warning signs and knew the bears stalked the shore this time of year but he didn't care.

How he'd walked twenty yards to open water and kept walking into the shallows until it was near the top of his boots. He pulled Wynn's canoe from his pocket and set it in the water. It windcocked into the onshore wind and faced the open sea of

Hudson Bay. Good. "Good, Wynn," he whispered. "You carved it true. Of course you did." How he pushed the little boat toward open water. But the tide was slack and the wind kept knocking the canoe back into his legs. It wouldn't go. "Hey, hey," he whispered. "It's okay, it's okay, you can go now. Please." It was almost desperate. How the boat turned sideways against the top of his boot and rested there. He stood in the shallows against the small waves and didn't move. He looked out into the bay where the line of the horizon was gray against gray. Sky and sea the same. A skein of geese. He closed his eyes. He smelled salt. He heard the rapid plaint of a gull. And then he picked up the canoe and held it in his hand and walked back into town.

Acknowledgments

Many people lent their energy and wisdom to the making of this book. To my first readers, Kim Yan, Lisa Jones, Helen Thorpe, Donna Gershten, Jay Heinrichs, and Mark Lough, I am deeply grateful. Your passion and ready insights were essential, as always. These books would not live without you.

Thanks to Jad Davenport for deep knowledge of the country and for sharing with me a crucial history. And to Jason Hicks, Steve Schon, Bobby Reedy, Mike Reedy, Billy Nutt, Cedar Farwell, Jay Mead, Silas Farwell, Sascha Steinway, Lyn Bixby, Mark Young, John French, Geordie Heller, and Becky Arnold, for their expertise. And to Kate Whalen for fuel. Lamar Simms provided invaluable help in understanding the law. And for all things medical, doctors Melissa Brannon and Mitchell Gershten were indispensable. Thanks to firefighter Jim Mason for relating in great detail the characteristics and awesome power of fire and to Marilee Rippy for introducing us. To Shawn Manzanares and Angela Lewark I am always grateful.

Thanks to my old friend Creigh Moffatt for telling me about her father's expedition up on the Dubawnt River and to Skip Pessl for sharing more of the story. Many years ago Peggy

ACKNOWLEDGMENTS

Keith and her daughter, Margaret Keith-Sagal, hosted a dinner in New Hampshire that provided the germ of this novel. Thanks for that evening and for so many others.

Thank you to the people of Peawanuk for your hospitality after a long river trip, to Kim for paddling with me, and to Lynn Cox, and Matt, and Jerry.

And thank you to the ones who ran the rivers, my paddling partners over the years, who shared with me the wildest and most beautiful country and who always had my back. This book is especially for you. Landis Arnold, Sascha Steinway, Andy Arnold, Roy Bailey, Newton Logan, Rafael Gallo, Adam Duerk, Peter Weingarten, Paul Bozuwa, Harold Schoeffler, Willy Kistler, John Mattson, John Jaycox, Dan Johnson, Chuck Behrensmeyer, Jay Mead, Billy Nutt—you are my brothers, always.

This book would not have been written without the encouragement and guidance of my extraordinary agent, David Halpern, and my brilliant editor, Jenny Jackson. You were both there from the first sentence, and to you both I raise a glass.

It is an honor and a privilege to know you all.